This book is dedicated to bloggers everywhere. The world is a big place and there's room in it for every voice.

Edited by Cynthia Shepp
www.cynthiashepp.com

Prologue: The Door

Tucked away in a small recess, around a corner and behind a vending machine, is a door. By today's standards it appears unusual. It is not exceptional in its shape or other dimensions, but it is distinctly different in a way that is difficult to define. The door is made of wood, as are many doors. The grain of the wood creates an intricate spiral pattern visible through the amber finish. In the nearly abandoned institutional setting, however, the wooden door seems out of place when compared with the more modern steel and glass sections of the edifice that contains it. The brass, bulb-style handle appears to be far out of place, an ornament from another time.

The broad, windowless door serves as the dead end of a short, dark alcove. There is no light to brighten this exaggerated cubby; no windows nearby and no glowing globe hanging from the ceiling. It is as if the architects intended it to be ignored. The door is almost hidden in plain sight. Although the nearby vending machine must certainly attract regular traffic, the floor in front of the door appears to be thick with the gray dust that always seems to coat the hallways of buildings usually referred to as institutions. It has the smell you recognize from the time you secretly found your way into the boiler room of your elementary school all those years ago. It is a smell that tells you that you are alone in a place entered rarely and only by necessity.

Centered directly above the door, mounted so that it points straight out from the wall, is a basic light fixture containing a single, bare, red bulb. The red light is not illuminated, nor does it appear to have been in quite some time. What could the red light be intended as a warning for? A swath of dim light from the nearby hallway reluctantly edges its way into the entryway. It is by this dim light that I am able to make out two details that had escaped my notice at first glance. On the wall to the left of the oddly imposing door is a switch in the down position. In the gloomy light I am also able to see that there is a single word stenciled on the door at about eye level. The letters are gold and of a font that appears to be quite old.

"Necropsy" it simply says. Behind the door is death, or at least this is where death used to be when this was a functioning hospital. Death may yet be awaiting me on the other side of this door.

The room behind the mysterious door is the old morgue. I tentatively reach out to try the knob, not sure if I really want it to turn. The brass handle refuses to budge and in my mind I feel a relief that I hope isn't apparent on my face. On a whim, I flip the switch to my left. Nothing happens. No sound from within the room. No red light suddenly ablaze above me. No blaring alarms to warn anyone of an intruder. What could the switch be for? As I look to the space at the bottom of the door expecting to see a sliver of light from within, I instead see something that seems to make my blood freeze in my veins. At first I am unsure if it is just a shadow, but as I bend down to look more closely, I see that it is indeed what I feared it might be.

A footprint, or rather, half of a footprint. The other half I assume is on the other side of the door. All that is visible is the imprint of a heel in the dust. It is barely visible, but a distinct impression is definitely there. Someone had entered this locked door in the very recent past.

The hospital hadn't been open, save for a few isolated outpatient offices in another wing, in five years. The one-hundred-year-old institution had been a victim of poor financial planning and, at the end, a scandal resulting from a contamination of the hospital's water system with the bacteria that causes Legionnaire's Disease. Some of the victims of that outbreak had no doubt had their autopsies performed in the room I now desperately knew I must find a way into. A week ago I could not have conceived of the series of events that caused me to question virtually everything I thought I knew about my life and brought me to this door.

1

The fog seemed appropriate, as if it were an ethereal chariot come down to carry his soul back to heaven. The cold, late April drizzle added to the misery of a funeral that no one had expected. A small, hastily constructed awning protected them as each person in turn filed past the casket and laid a rose upon it, whispering a few words of good-bye. Cooper put his hand on his friend's shoulder and gave a brief squeeze, "Well Dave, I never expected to see you again so soon, or in these circumstances. I'm sorry."

Dave looked his friend in the eye for a moment before looking away into the distance. "Thanks Coop. First Chuck's dad and now mine. This has been a bad year. We're too young to be losing our parents already," he replied in little more than a rough whisper. Cooper paused for a moment before placing his rose on the casket and walking over to join the others. Although the cemetery was crowded with mourners, the four men stood out as they gathered together.

In our minds we are *The Golden Boys*. At least that's how we think of ourselves. Not because of any special qualities we have, or because of any of us has led a particularly charmed life. We are four fairly normal, middle-aged men who have been together our entire lives. We can't remember a time when we didn't know each other. We want to think we're special. Like all men our age, we still believe that if we had the time to train we could become professional athletes or crime-fighting superheroes. Despite a sprinkle of gray hair beginning to show or abs that aren't as defined as we'd like to imagine, we still fantasize that we can turn the ladies' heads.

We'd dubbed ourselves *The Golden Boys* when we were barely past puberty. The name was borrowed from a skit on a short-lived show called *Fridays* that featured two pseudo-professional wrestlers clad in capes and gold bikini briefs. Together they would shout their motto in unison, "We're young, we're tough, and we're good looking!" Needless to say, we quickly adopted that motto and shouted it whenever we were together. We still do if we've been drinking. We also developed a secret handshake that we still greet each other with to this day.

Our most sacred and enduring ritual is *The Walk*. We grew up in suburbia. Everytown, USA. Identical houses and identical yards as far as the eye could see. A corner store we could walk to. Four guys in four consecutive houses. We are all about the same age from average, middle-class families. Our ritual, when the weather was willing, and sometimes when it wasn't, was *The Walk*. The 'walk around the block'. In the beginning it was rarely spoken or suggested, it just sort of happened. Any time of day or night it could happen. As kids, after we finished swimming or building a fort, or when we got older, after a night out on the town. We would just walk and talk. We knew every foot of that walk like the back of our hands. We knew who lived in every house, all fifty-six of them, fifty-eight after they added the two down at the end. It was the best neighborhood in the world as far as we knew, and we felt like we were the kings of it.

The Walk is still our ritual, but it's changed. None of us live in the old neighborhood anymore and our reasons for visiting it are almost gone. In our eyes though, the old neighborhood is unchanged. A time capsule of our childhood. As adult men now, we still go back to the neighborhood and take *The Walk*. We walk down the middle of the street at night and we point to every house and talk about the memory of a childhood friend, or the time it caught fire, or what tragedy befell the old folks, who weren't so old when we rang their doorbell and ran. For three of the four of us, the neighborhood doesn't belong to us anymore. Our parents have passed away or divorced and sold our childhood homes. But still we walk. The first time this year when one of our parents passed away, we again returned to the neighborhood after calling hours and took *The Walk*. After today's funeral we again drove to the old neighborhood, parked the car at the corner store, and walked by our childhood, wondering where it went. Someday when the first of us passes away, I imagine the others will take *The Walk*, carrying our friend's casket around the block, one last time.

We walked down the street in our old neighborhood, unaware that our arrival there was observed. As we walked in the dim light of the streetlamps we were quiet at first, our usual jocularity taken from us by the day's solemn events. Although we were still dressed in our suits, we were at ease as we walked. The old neighborhood did that to us.

As always, uncomfortable with silence, I spoke up first. "This is definitely weird having two of our parents die within a year. The rest of them have got to be feeling very nervous all of a sudden."

Cliff sighed, "It does make you all of a sudden begin to wonder if anyone is safe. I can't imagine anything happening to my parents, but your dad was only five years older than mine."

"I know," replied Dave. "My dad always worked so hard. I never imagined he'd stop."

Chuck, the quietest throughout the day, spoke up, "When my mom passed away, we expected it, but my dad's sudden heart attack, and now your dad's death, Dave. What is going on?" We all moved to the side, single file to let a car pass by. The accompanying breeze gave a momentary chill as we moved back into the middle of the quiet street.

"Well," I said, "maybe all those years of neighborhood cookouts and beer drinking are finally taking their toll." I paused momentarily to pick up a pop can and toss it into the nearest garbage can as we passed. The houses all looked the same as they always had. Some of the names on the mailboxes had changed, but most had not.

"I wonder if the new people in the neighborhood question why four guys in suits are walking around their neighborhood at night."

"Fuck'em," Cliff replied. "It's not their neighborhood. It's ours."

No one disagreed. It was how we all felt. We walked on in silence a little further with only the soft mutterings of the neighborhood at night to interrupt our thoughts. Occasionally someone would break the silence to comment on what they had heard about the neighbor whose house we were passing or to talk about a childhood friend who no longer lived there.

"I'm getting tired of all this depressing stuff. I could use a beer. Anybody else?" It was not a question that needed to be asked. That ritual was as much a part of our relationship as *The Walk*. Our destination, O'Brien's Pub, was as much a given as everything else.

We are creatures of habit when we come together. Although we've moved out of our neighborhood and only get together a few times a year as a group, our relationship is what it always was, an unusual lifetime bond that has grown with us over the years. We still tease and taunt each other as if we are adolescents. Gone, however, is the malice of adolescent teasing, replaced by gentle chiding about the things that we know will eventually be common to us all, gray hair or balding, pot bellies, and vasectomies. As we sat at the bar that night, we all seemed stunned by how abruptly reality had stolen our sense of security in the world. Although we are all grown men, the idea that our parents, the people who had always made us feel safe and still did, could be gone so suddenly, left the four of us to reconsider the idyllic framework of the world that was embedded in our minds. Our childhood had been a safe one filled with summer days exploring forests and ponds, imagining we were modern day Tom Sawyers and Huck Finns, a distant cry from today's need for parents to be on the verge of paranoia whenever their children leave the house.

2

I was a man who thought I knew who I was, where I had been, and where I was going in life. The week to come would drastically alter the utopian perception I had of my life. I had a successful private practice as a therapist, specializing in pyromaniacs and children who had been victims of cults. By the age of thirty-four I had published two books, and occasionally earned a nice chunk of change as a guest speaker at conferences in my areas of expertise. I was married and had three beautiful children. In general, life was good. It felt like I had recreated the All-American, apple-pie life I had grown up in. That was my goal for my children to enjoy their childhood as much as I had.

Outside of my love for my career and family, my recreational passion was chess. I love the complexity, the strategy, the way a chess game mimics real life. At every turn there's a choice and with every choice, potential success or devastating consequences that could cost you everything. I think of almost every life decision as if it were a chess decision. *If I make this move, what will be the ripple effects of it two or three steps down the road?* Occasionally I compete in local tournaments and usually I'm happy to make a good showing against one of the national tournament players.

One thing I'm not very happy about is death. The ultimate checkmate. I don't like it when it happens to people I know and I'm especially annoyed with the idea that it could happen to me. In all other regards I think of myself as the model of mental health, a well-balanced role model for my patients. In regards to death however, I have a pathological hang up. I can't admit that I will find myself taking the big dirt nap one day. Secretly, in the back of my mind, I want to believe that by sheer force of will I'll live forever with my current mental and physical faculties unchanged.

My best friend's parent's deaths had shaken me more than I was willing to admit. Although I wasn't as close to my parents as most people, I still wasn't ready to say good-bye to them forever. Until Chuck and Dave's fathers had passed away during the last seven months, I had never experienced the death of someone that close to me. Fortunately, my three friends appeared as shaken as I did, and as always, we went through everything in our lives together, whether it was by phone, e-mail, Facebook message, or by sharing a drunken weekend.

3

Dave picked me up in his father's old van. We were headed to the old neighborhood, to his father's house, to begin the arduous task of cleaning out his home of the last thirty years. I had spent half of my childhood here, but it seemed foreign to me now that Colt was gone. His name wasn't really Colt, but we called him that because, as kids, we thought he bore a resemblance to a character on a TV show we watched.

Still, being in the company of my lifelong friend,

Dave, was always enjoyable. I have probably known Dave since he was about three days old. I'm one year and one day older than him. Our parents lived two houses apart and were always friends. That being the case, I'm fairly certain that when his mom came home from the hospital with the new baby, my mom scooped me up and went over to visit her friend and her new offspring. His nickname is Gooby.

Of course the most obvious question is, how did he get the nickname Gooby? That started when we were all about ten or eleven years old. At the end of our street was a police station. Each winter the snow plows would create huge mountains of snow on the edges of the parking lot when they cleared it. As boys, Gooby, Cliff, Chuck, and I would bundle ourselves up in our snow clothes and head down to the police station. The police had grown to know us from our frequent trips into the lobby to get drinks of water and pick up the cool bumper stickers they gave out.

When we got to the snowy police station parking lot, we would play a reverse *King of the Hill* kind of game. We'd climb to the top of one of those towering piles of snow and one of us would expectorate a big, green goober upon the top of the hill. As soon as someone said, "GO!" we would battle to push each other onto the top of the mountain.

Gooby, as a ten-year-old, had the physical build of a newborn deer, all spindly bones and no muscle mass whatsoever. Needless to say, he lost our prepubescent manhood contest more often than not and ended up with a frozen goober stuck to his parka—and so a nickname was born. Gooby is the quintessential nice guy and the glue that holds our little group together. Whenever any of us has anything serious going on in our personal lives such as tragedies, triumphs or elective surgeries—we confide in him, even though we know he tells the other three everything when we're not there.

Dave 'Gooby' Richards wasn't sure who he was, where he had been, or where he was going in life. Despite his lifelong friendship with the three of us, the recent death of his father had taken away his true best friend. They had worked together every weekend. In addition to his full-time job, Gooby spent his days off helping his father, who was a drywall contractor.

Although his life wasn't what he had planned on at high school graduation, he was getting by all right. Prior to the events of this past week, he had successfully settled down with his high school sweetheart, less successfully divorced eight years later, and maintained a lucrative, but monotonous, career as an Information Technology Manager (translation: computer geek) for an enormous hospital system. Outside of work he was still a computer geek. His hobby was those online role-playing games where you paid to play and could link up with other online gamers. Occasionally, he even amused himself by using his computer skills to create very clever pictures of the rest of *The Golden Boys* in very compromising positions.

Gooby wasn't your typical computer geek though. When he wasn't online, he was working out. Most likely he could easily kick the asses of all his online friends at once. Despite the combination of brains and brawn that women seemed to love, he had been a little gun shy about jumping back into the dating pool after his divorce. He had gotten plenty of offers of fix-ups and blind dates as soon as word of his separation got out, but losing his first love was something he wasn't getting over very easily. He wasn't sure where he was going in life, but he had settled into a comfortable rut for now. It was a rut that was occasionally filled with whiskey or his grandfather's homemade wine.

We pulled into the driveway of his father's old Cape Cod-style home. The home he had kept after his divorce. We paused before getting out and Gooby broke the momentary silence. "Thanks for coming along with me, Coop. I don't think I could do this by myself."

"No problem," I replied, "It's too bad Cliff and Chuck couldn't come too. We could have grabbed some beers and made a day of it."

Goob laughed. "The way Chuck handles his alcohol; I think he'd probably be more harm than help. Why the United States Army lets that guy try to talk people into joining is beyond me. Besides, I don't think I'd do very well with a few beers in me right now."

We got out of the car and walked up the driveway. The pleasant spring breeze and sunshine did little to lift our mood. Although it was just a house, it seemed to emanate stillness; an emptiness that the other homes in the neighborhood didn't have. I know it was in my imagination, but maybe it is possible that our homes take on an energy or personality from us. This house just felt empty and cold. I couldn't imagine anyone other than Gooby's dad filling it with life.

I paused on the step as Dave fumbled with his keys. I looked around at the old neighborhood with a feeling of nostalgia. There were a few minor changes to some of the homes, but by and large it was where I had grown up, two doors from where we stood now. It wasn't my parents' divorce that had broken my heart. That I expected. It was losing the opportunity to come home that I missed the most.

Although the house had only been empty a week, it felt as it were another world, frozen in time. His keys and unopened mail still sat on the small table by the door. Everything was still in its place. It was a snapshot of the last day of a man's life.

"Well, where do we start?" I asked.

After letting out a heavy sigh that reflected his heavy heart, Dave replied, "Well, we don't have to do too much. Just the important stuff. I'm hiring an estate company to just come in and sell what's left after I clear out all of his personal things. I'll go through his desk, computer, and financial files. Do you mind clearing all the food out of the refrigerator and kitchen? There's no need to save anything."

I grabbed a big, gray, plastic garbage can out of the garage and brought it into the kitchen, setting it next to the avocado-green refrigerator. However, the hideous refrigerator wasn't so bad when it sat next to the orange-striped wallpaper that covered the kitchen. Why the hell our parents had stopped redecorating after 1979 always puzzled me. Goob's dad was a man who didn't put on airs though. Decorating wasn't something that he was likely to have spent a lot of time worrying about, unlike his slightly anal-retentive son.

The inside of the fridge was stocked, as are most single guys' refrigerators, with lots of beer, condiments, and not much else. "Hey Goob," I shouted to the next room. "Your dad had some nice steaks in the freezer, quite a bit of beer, and a bottle of wine in the fridge. Do you want me to save those?"

He walked in and looked over the contents of the fridge. "Don't save the steaks; I would feel kind of weird eating his old food. Save the beer and wine though. It would kind of seem like I was sharing a drink with him one last time. We always used to stop by his house after work on Saturdays in the summer and have a couple beers on the deck. I grew up here. We'll sit out on the deck when we're done and take care of those beers. It's going to be hard to sell this place."

Goob seemed lost in his thoughts for a moment. I was fearful of breaking the silence, but then he did it for me. "You know, even though a house is just bricks, mortar, and wood, when it's filled with your memories, it almost feels like a living, breathing part of you."

I didn't have a reply to this. I'd never suffered a loss like he had. Eager to take his mind off the reason we were there, I interrupted. "Hey Goob, I know it's only nine in the morning, but you wanna crack open a couple beers now? We don't have anything else to do today, right?"

His mood brightened quickly, as if he had shaken himself out of his thoughts. "Sure, why not? Let's not get too carried away though. My dad wasn't much of a wine drinker. I wonder where he got this," he said, looking at the bottle of Merlot in the refrigerator.

I picked it up for a moment, noticing the gift tag tied to the neck. "It must have been a Christmas gift from someone," I said. "It says it's from the paperboy. Damn, I need to get a better paperboy. I didn't get anything but a freakin' calendar."

He opened his beer with a twist of the cap and said, "C'mon, let's get back to work. We'll never get out of here if we just stand around talking."

I went back to work, throwing away food that would never be eaten. Dave returned to the other room and I could hear him rummaging around in his father's desk. I continued to discard what looked like boxes and cans of food that were almost as old as I was when I heard Dave say, "Huh. This is weird."

I walked into the other room to see what had aroused his curiosity. "What is it?" I asked.

"It's a motel room ticket," Dave replied. "It's from someplace called 'Shaheen's Motel'. I wonder where that is. I don't remember my dad ever going anywhere by that name."

"Is your dad's computer still online?" I asked, "You could use the phone number and do a reverse look-up to find out where it is."

He responded with our usual sophomoric sarcasm, "Hey, that's a good idea. You're not as stupid as Cliff and Chuck make you out to be."

"Talk about the pot calling the kettle black," I fired back. "Those guys are lucky they don't have to ride a short bus to work every day." As I said, our adolescent instincts haven't slowed with age, and I don't expect they ever will.

Dave quickly logged onto his father's computer. Out of habit, I pretended to avert my eyes as he typed in the password. This bit of modern-day politeness was hardly necessary as Dave's fingers navigated the keyboard faster than my eye could follow. He found the phone company website and hastily typed in the phone number from the ticket stub. A web page with a log cabin flanked by two pine trees popped up. Dave read aloud, "Shaheen's Motel, Tupper Lake, New York."

"Hmm…that's weird," I said, "Tupper Lake is near where my family used to go camping when I was a kid, but we never stayed in a motel. Remember? You went up there with me once when we were kids."

Dave rolled his eyes. "How could I forget? You ditched me half the time to go make out in the woods with that girl you met."

I couldn't help but laugh at that. It was true. We never noticed this when we were younger, but once you hit about thirteen or fourteen, the campground suddenly became a meat market for all the teenagers who were sure they were too cool for camping with the family, but were forced to go anyway.

"Hey Goob, in all seriousness, maybe there are some things about your dad you don't know. Why don't you call your mom? Maybe they went there before you were born or something. That would explain why you don't remember it. Judging from the looks of the place, I can see why your dad would want to forget it."

He paused in thought for a moment. "No, no, I can't ask my mom. They're divorced. What if this motel ticket is from a time he was meeting someone else?"

After a minutes' thought and some aimless rifling through papers, I had an idea. "Why not just call the motel? Tell them that your dad passed away, you're getting his affairs in order, and that you just want to make sure he doesn't have any outstanding bills owed. You can ask them when he last stayed there!"

Gooby accepted the idea because at that point our curiosity about the origin of the motel ticket was a welcome distraction. As he dialed, I forgot about the events of the last few days and spent a minute mentally patting myself on the back for being so brilliant. I knew it wasn't exactly the detective work of *CSI: New York,* but I allowed myself that indulgent little fantasy as he made the call.

Dave concluded his call. "Now this is strange. They said he's been there twice in the last year, but the bills were paid. What the hell was he doing in Tupper Lake, and why didn't I know he was gone? I worked with him every weekend. If he was gone for a few days, I'm sure I'd have noticed."

Again, using all the deductive instincts I had gleaned from a lifetime of watching cop shows, I said, "Did you get the dates he was there? There had to be times he was out of town but told you he was going somewhere else."

"Yeah, here they are. The last was just a week and a half ago. That was when I was in Chicago for that conference. The other time was last summer. July."

"Hmm…when in July?" I asked.

"It looks like it was from July 13th to the 15th," Goob said.

"You know what?" I said. "That was the weekend we all got together at my cottage. This may seem crazy, but it looks like he was intentionally going there when you weren't apt to notice." I realize I sound like a dork, but sometimes I actually do use words like 'apt' in conversation.

With no answer readily apparent, we decided to get back to our work and talk about his dad's mysterious trips to Tupper Lake later. As morning turned to afternoon and one or two beers turned into three or four, we realized that we probably weren't going anywhere for the rest of the day—or evening for that matter. We called Cliff and asked him to grab Chuck and a case of OV Splits and head over after work. Gooby decided that eating those steaks wouldn't be so bad after all.

"Hey Coop, are you sure your wife won't mind you staying with me tonight?" Goob asked.

"Not at all," I replied. "I'm comforting my grief-stricken friend. You need me. How could she say no to that? Besides, I took the week off from work. I don't have anywhere else to be." Cliff and Chuck arrived shortly thereafter and the serious matter of drinking began. Regardless of the reason, whenever we get together, we're happy to be in each other's company, and alcohol was usually involved.

4

Late afternoon turned into evening. It was dusk by the time we had finished cleaning up the remains of our meal. "Hey, wanna take a walk?" Cliff asked. As usual no one even considered any other course of action. It was what we did. *The Walk*. We all grabbed a cold beer and headed out into the brisk evening. Cliff took the lead. "So Goob, you ever think of keeping your dad's place?"

Dave pondered this for a moment. 'You know, I did think of it, but I'd have to talk about it with my sister. She's entitled to half."

"Maybe you could let her have all the life insurance and stocks and you keep the house," I chipped in.

"You know, we talked about it," he replied. "With her living in Connecticut, she has no interest in the house, and she's certainly not in need of money."

Chuck interrupted that thought. "Hey guys, check out the chick coming down the Henderson's driveway up there."

A lifetime of male reflexes kicked in and we all nearly got whiplash from how quickly we moved our heads. It wasn't the sulky looking 'goth' teens smoking on the corner he had noticed. Chuck's radar had detected a very attractive, dark-haired, voluptuous, thirty-something woman approaching the end of what must be her driveway, apparently to check her mailbox. She seemed to hesitate and stood flipping through her mail as we approached.

Never at a loss for words, Cliff spoke up, "What's a nice lady like you doing out here near dark? You never know what kind of trouble you might run into."

"I take it your name is Trouble," she responded with a sly smile.

Cliff Thomas was *The Golden Boy*. In high school he was the star athlete, the prom king, and everything else important in the world of adolescence. He was high school royalty. It didn't hurt him any that he was tall, blonde, and blue-eyed either. The rest of us ended up as his best friends by proximity. Four guys in four consecutive houses. A lifetime of experiences had bonded us together. Without the coincidence of our shared neighborhood, we likely would have never been friends. With his All-American good looks and his All-Star athletic talents, he traveled in different social circles than the rest of us when we were inside the walls of average American high school. When school hours were done however, and we were on our home turf, he was just as big a doofus as the rest of us. Maybe the rest of us were a little jealous, or perhaps we wanted to keep his ego from getting too big, but we seemed to take a little extra delight in knocking him down a few pegs with our teasing. He always took it in stride with the confidence of someone who knew that the best revenge was living well.

His athletic ability had paved the way for an athletic scholarship. It wasn't to a major college, but free tuition to Elmira University was certainly a major perk when you consider the cost of college these days. Unfortunately, Cliff's dreams of athletic fame were not to be. The university was kind enough to continue his scholarship after he blew out his knee in a pick-up basketball game. Now he was a successful physical therapist, helping athletes and former athletes crippled by the games that brought them fame. He was married, had two very athletic children, and lived in an affluent suburb. By all appearances, he was still the All-American boy.

His only flaw as far as we could tell was his enduring addiction to Halls cherry cough drops. As a kid he had allergies and was always sucking the syrupy sweet cough drops because they helped alleviate his nasal congestion. Apparently they were addicting because he was still sucking them now. If you were within arm's length, you could smell his breath, and maybe it was just my imagination, but I thought his teeth were beginning to take on a pinkish tinge. I have no idea how his wife tolerates kissing him and I hope that's something I never find the answer to.

"Do we look like trouble?" Cliff answered. "We're just four nice young men keeping an eye on our neighborhood. Sort of like the neighborhood watch."

"If his name is Trouble—who are the rest of you?" she asked. We all introduced ourselves and she explained that she had moved here to take care of her aging, ailing parents. Her name was Maria. As she spoke a cool night breeze, that had just begun to stir, blew a strand of light auburn hair across her face. She smoothed it back behind her ear with her left hand. I would bet my next paycheck that we all noted, with interest, that her left hand was without rings of any kind.

"Well, welcome to the neighborhood," Chuck said. "Don't worry—with us around, you couldn't be safer here."

"Thanks boys. It's a bit chilly for me to be out here without a coat. It was nice meeting you." We had all already noted that it was a bit chilly out here for Maria. We gave a polite "good-bye/it was nice to meet you" and she headed back up the drive to her door.

As we continued to amble casually down the street, I caught both Chuck and Gooby sneaking a glance at Maria's back as she walked up her driveway. After we had gotten out of earshot, Chuck said, "Well she's a nice addition to the neighborhood. I think I may be coming over to visit you a lot more often, Goob."

"Hey, I'm single too, and suddenly I think I may just feel like living in my dad's old house," Dave replied.

"No way," said Chuck. "I saw her first. I got dibs." Chuck had invoked the age-old guy code of dibs. We never worried too much when Chuck called dibs. It rarely resulted in anything for him.

As we continued our walk, the last glowing embers of sunset disappeared and night began to settle in. We rounded a bend and I heard the idling of a large engine nearby. What appeared to be a large SUV was parked by the side of the road a couple of houses ahead. *A suburban mom probably dropping off her kid for a sleepover*, I thought. As we approached, the idling engine roared to life and the SUV, a Hummer I thought, seemed to leap from the curb and barreled towards us. I froze for a split-second. Goob and I dove for the ditch to the side of the road, but the Hummer was much closer to Cliff and Chuck. I landed in the ditch next to Gooby. As I rose to look at the rear of the Hummer I saw Cliff sprawled on the pavement, while in one fluid motion Chuck rose to one knee with a gun pointed at the back of the vehicle as it sped away into the darkness. Without flinching, Chuck fired a single shot that ricocheted off some part of the vehicle—without slowing its escape.

"Holy shit, Chuck!" Cliff exclaimed. "What the hell was that?"

"Shut up. Get up if you can. We've got to get back to the house without being seen. Quick, follow me."

To say that the three of us were stunned by the fact that our lifelong friend, the one whom we have always had such little regard for, had pulled out a gun and fired off a shot like he knew what he was doing, was an understatement of gargantuan proportions. The fact that we were so taken aback, coupled with the fact that Chuck suddenly seemed like he was in charge, led us to follow him like ducklings after their mother. He led us on a labyrinthine path through the backyards of our neighborhood, carefully avoiding security lights as we wound our way towards Gooby's house. In the distance, the wail of sirens began and quickly grew closer.

"So Chuck, when exactly did you turn into Batman?"

"Coop! This isn't the time," he hissed at me. "We need to get inside before we're spotted."

Chuck Stinson was always the tag-along little brother to the older three of us. He was the youngest by two years and was moderately vertically challenged, but definitely not dwarf-like. Unfortunately for him, these traits also made him the group scapegoat for practical jokes. As Gooby had, Chuck had spent his early adulthood working out so that no one would kick sand in his face again. Chuck now looked like he could probably kick all of our asses. Maybe that's what he wanted. If there is any justice in the world, Chuck will one day own a billion-dollar corporation, hire the rest of us, and then fire us just out of spite for the abuse we heaped upon him when we were younger. He had three older brothers of his own, but he wisely chose the three of us as his role models. He had been a bit aimless after high school. He was smart enough to earn a scholarship to an engineering university, but not mature enough to buckle down to his studies when he got there. Scholarship revoked, college career over. Hello U.S. Army! Having spent twelve years in the Army, he was no doubt a much more mature man than he had been as an adolescent. Despite this, he and the rest of us immediately reverted to our old roles when we got together, and that was a battle

Chuck was never going to win. I had a feeling that had just changed.

After we safely got back to Goob's dad's house, grabbed another beer, and settled into the living room, the questions started. Dave said, "Dude! That was totally whack! Why the hell are you carrying a gun? I thought you just did recruiting stuff for the Army."

Chuck paused before replying, "Goob, you're in your thirties and you just used the words 'dude' and 'whack'. If you do it again, I may be forced to shoot you."

We all laughed for a few seconds. For some reason unknown to the rest of us Goob's vocabulary seemed stuck in our teenage years and that habit always earned a little ridicule from the rest of us.

Chuck went on, "Well, I'm not supposed to tell you this, so you can't say anything to anyone." We all nodded our consent. "I've been a part of the Homeland Security Task Force for the past four years. I would seriously get my ass kicked if I had to explain to the cops or my superiors why I fired a shot in a residential neighborhood when I was off duty."

Cliff piped in, "Don't you think you went a little overboard with that shove you gave me? I'm sure I would have gotten myself out of the way."

"Are you kidding?' I said. "You're drunk, you're old, and you've got a serious boiler going. You've got the reflexes of a sloth at this point." We all laughed. Except Cliff—he gets pissed at stuff like that.

"Chuck, don't you think you got a little carried away firing at the truck like that?" Goob asked. "I mean, it could have just been some stupid kid who forgot to turn on his headlights or some drunk driver."

"I don't think so," Chuck replied. "Think about it. That's a big vehicle with a big engine. If he had been driving up the street, we would have heard him coming before we rounded the corner. Also, even if it were getting dark, he would have seen us when he got close. He was accelerating and never hit the brakes. In fact, he gunned the engine after we dove out of the way. Whoever it was, they were trying to run us down."

Cliff, who seemed to be enjoying a good beer buzz, said, "You're nuts, Chuck. You've been doing too much of that spy shit. Not everything is a conspiracy. I think you just wanted to show off your big gun. This is our neighborhood. Why would anyone want to run us down?"

I couldn't resist the big gun reference. "Yeah Chuck, I think that big gun is your way of compensating for your little wiener." We all laughed and Chuck blushed. Or at least we thought he did. His cheeks were always red. He had that medical condition, whatever it was called, that made his cheeks always look like he just came in from the cold.

"Get lost with that psychological crap, Coop. I think you went into psychology just to prove you weren't nuts," Chuck answered.

One beer to take the edge off the adrenaline that was screaming through our bodies after the near miss had turned into two, three, and four—to the point we lost count.

Considering the amount of beer we'd had, and that

this was Goob's house now, we made the smart decision to just sleep here tonight. Our brains may not have matured much in the last fifteen years, but unfortunately our bodies had. We grew tired from the day's events and the amount of alcohol in our systems. Everyone decided to turn in.

I'm not a pacifist and I don't begrudge anyone their right to bear arms—or arm bears for that matter—but I've also never been a gun person either. The extent of my gun use is pretty much limited to the handful of times that my cousin and I would take our B.B. guns into the field behind my house and pretend that we might have a chance to hit a wild rabbit or bird that crossed our path. Those were intense stakeouts for sure. Needless to say that although I trusted Chuck, it still made me nervous to know there was a loaded weapon in the house. I'm mean really—what if Chuck started sleepwalking with his gun and killed us all? Although crazy little thoughts like that are anxiety-provoking, they are not more powerful than a six-pack of beer in a thirty-six-year-old body. Eventually, against my better judgment, I succumbed to sleep.

If I didn't have a bladder the size of a pea, I might not have awoken at all. Fortunately, nature called to me loud and clear through the fog in my brain. As I rolled myself off the couch and began to stumble through the darkness to the bathroom, I felt groggy. Too groggy. And something smelled funny. I had spent the evening in the company of three grown men who seemed to delight in their ability to produce enough methane gas to rip a Texas-sized hole in the ozone directly above us, so a foul smell was not totally unexpected. This smell was different though. This smell wasn't bad bodily-functions gas—it was the skunky smell of natural gas.

There was a leak in the house. Forgetting my need

for a different type of leak, I immediately stumbled into the kitchen and opened a window. I clutched the windowsill, gasping to suck the cool, damp night air into my lungs. A few deep breaths cleared my head. At least as much as it could. As I shook the cobwebs out of my brain, I remembered the guys. I had to wake them and get them out without anyone so much as flicking on a light switch. In a house full of natural gas, any spark—electrical or otherwise—could set off an explosion that would kill us all.

I tiptoed as quietly as I could through the downstairs, opening windows and doors, hoping that if I let in enough fresh air I could avoid being blown to smithereens if one of my drunken compadres woke up and turned on a light. (Yes, sometimes I actually use the word 'compadres' in my head.) After this was done I crept up the stairs, cringing at what seemed to be painfully loud creaks as I set my foot upon every stair. Who to wake first? I wasn't even sure who was in which room. I don't really remember everyone heading to bed. I had just sort of dropped off to sleep on the couch. Later I'll have to look in the mirror to see if those stupid bastards had put food coloring on my face again. Ever since Goob's bachelor party, when I had *allegedly* initiated drawing on the unconscious Chuck's face with a permanent marker, I had been the target of revenge attempts.

The gas smell wasn't so bad up here. I think the fresh air from downstairs had helped matters. My nerves were on edge, sobering me up a lot faster than any amount of coffee could have. I crept into the first room on the right, unsure if I should wake Cliff or try to open a window. I chose to go for the window, hoping that if I let in some air, I'd decrease the risk if one of the other guys woke up and hit a light switch.

I slowly and softly stepped through the doorway, cringing with fear at each step. This old house seemed to be a virtual minefield of creaky floorboards that echoed loudly with every step. I'm sure my tension was amplifying the sound in my mind, but thinking that didn't help me relax. As I crept as slowly and as softly as possible past the end of the bed to the window, I felt a sudden *crack* and an excruciating shot of pain as my pinky toe caught the corner of the dresser. I bit down hard on my lip to keep from crying out. I felt a trickle of blood as my incisor broke the soft, thin surface of my lip. If I wasn't alert enough before, I was now. Limping, I made it the last three steps to the window. As I fumbled with the latches at the top of the window, I heard the sheets move behind me.

"Who is that? What the fuck are you doing?" As always, Cliff had a gift with language that was a magnet for the ladies.

"Shhhhhh! It's me. Quiet. Listen, we gotta get out of here. There's a gas leak." Cliff was obviously still muddled from the evening's alcohol and possibly the natural gas.

"Coop, what the hell are you talking about? Where are my glasses?" In the moonlight from the window I could see his hand begin to reach for the bedside lamp. I took a step and leapt across the bed, literally tackling him and knocking his arm down against the nightstand.

"Cliff! Are you *listening*? There's gas in the house! You can't turn on a light! Stop it! Stop hitting me!" Cliff didn't understand. He was hitting me. Why are drunk people so stupid? These were the thoughts that rushed through my head as I heard footsteps in the hallway. Goob came in first and immediately flicked on the switch by the door. As the room was immediately ablaze with light I clutched onto Cliff, expecting to feel my body torn asunder or engulfed in flames.

"Hey, if you guys were going to go all *Brokeback Mountain*, why didn't you invite me?' Gooby quipped. I would have rolled my eyes if I didn't think it would cause an explosion.

"Goob, there's a gas leak," I said. "We have to get out of here. Don't you smell that?"

Chuck ambled in, rubbing his eyes. "Hey guys, why didn't you wake me up for the orgy? Cliff, I'm disappointed. I thought I was your special guy."

Goob appeared to have his wits about him a bit more than the other two. He had been working on his tolerance level like it was a job. "No, you guys, he's right. I smell gas."

Finally relieved to have someone else cut through the inane banter I said, "Duh! Shut off the light, you moron. Even an electrical spark can set off an explosion."

We all managed to get ourselves out of the house without further incident. As we stood on the front lawn Cliff called the gas company from his cell phone. The gas company truck arrived fairly soon and the technician found the leak using some sort of Geiger counter type of device. I was pleased that he acknowledged my obvious brilliance in opening as many windows as possible. The gas company guy, Cosmo, told us that the leak was from a valve attached to the furnace. I knew his name was Cosmo because it was tattooed on the side of his neck. He said that either someone had whacked the hell out of it with a hammer a few times, or someone had opened it intentionally.

That sure as hell sobered us up in a hurry. "Goob, are you sure you sure you never hit that valve? Maybe when you were working over there or something?" I asked.

"No," he replied. "That's way over in the corner behind the furnace. I'm never over there unless I'm changing the filter, and I haven't done that in months." We waited outside in the damp, cool night air as the gas company guys closed the valves, checked for other leaks, and tested the air in the house. A short while later Cosmo walked up, handed Dave a new furnace filter, and gave us the okay to return to the house.

As we all sat down around the kitchen table, Dave put on some coffee. Chuck spoke up. "That's twice tonight someone has tried to kill us. Now do you guys believe that the truck was not just some stupid driver?"

Cliff responded first, "Still, either one could have been an accident. A driver who forgot his lights, Goob hitting the furnace valve with a two by four."

"Yeah, but two accidents in one night that nearly kills all four of us? There is no way our luck is that bad," Dave said. "I'm with Chuck on this one—especially so soon after my Dad died. This is weird."

"Should we tell the police?" I wondered aloud.

Again, Chuck responded with an air of authority that we were all getting more comfortable letting him have. "Tell the police what? That a bad driver almost hit us and that Goob had a gas leak? There's not enough to prove someone is out to get us. We're going to have to watch our own backs for the next few days and look for anything suspicious, especially you, Goob. It happened at your dad's house. It's possible that you're the target and they're not after all of us."

Dave looked a little startled at this last proclamation. "Thanks Chuck, that's very reassuring. Can I borrow your gun?"

By the time we finished our modern day *Knights of The Roundtable* over coffee it was five a.m. There was no point in returning to bed. I didn't have to go to work, but I did have to return to my family sometime. Well, my second family. Despite being married and having kids, I still felt like these three guys were my first family. Together over thirty years, I had confided things in these men that my parents or my wife never knew. Such was the respect we had for each other.

When I was nine years old and wanted to run away from home because I was tired of my parents drinking and fighting, I went to Dave. We developed a plan where I would live in the shed behind his house and he would bring me food. I was still going to go to school every day of course. My nine-year-old brain still hadn't developed the capacity to appreciate that home and school could cross each other's path if need be.

When I was fourteen years old with my first girlfriend, I went to Cliff for advice on how to tactfully make my big move when we were alone. It worked. Cliff knew his shit when it came to girls, even then.

When I was twenty-two and overwhelmingly depressed because my girlfriend of two years had broken up with me and I had bombed my first attempt at the grad school entry exam all in the same week, Chuck was there to drink a beer with me and remind me that it was just a girl and just a test. For all the verbal abuse and mocking we heap upon each other, we have an unspoken respect built through a lifetime of saving each other's asses when we get in a tight spot.

Dave whipped up some eggs, bacon, and more coffee. He was always playing the host when we were at his house. Between his cooking and how immaculately clean he kept his house, we had often accused him of having some hidden gay tendencies. The rest of the morning we only talked a little about the supposed attempts on our lives. After breakfast I got dressed and prepared to head home. Chuck agreed to stay with Dave for another day and night. Cliff would take the next day. Dave needed help cleaning out his dad's house anyway and we figured he didn't want to be alone.

"Guys, I see what you're doing and I appreciate it," he said. "Chuck, if you can't stay tomorrow night—can't you at least leave your gun?"

"No way, Goob. If someone gets shot with that gun and I didn't fire it, I'm going to jail no matter what the reason. Besides, you're probably more likely to pee your pants than pull the trigger," Chuck replied.

We all laughed at that and Dave didn't argue. The four of us gathered on the driveway as Cliff and I prepared to leave. The events of last night seemed a lot less threatening in the morning sunshine. As always, we briefly joined in the four-way secret handshake that we had started as kids. As grown men it felt a little silly doing a secret handshake, but it would have felt a lot sillier not to.

5

Although I had only left about twenty-four hours ago, it felt as if I had been gone a lifetime. I don't think I had ever been so happy to be home. Unfortunately, my family wasn't there to greet me. My wife, Christine, was at work. I gave her a quick call to check in and to get my *honey-do* list.

My three boys were off at school. I had my suburban palace to myself. After nearly losing my life not once, but twice, overnight, I really wanted my family. Ah well, at least I had some time to mow my lawn. When I'm stressed out nothing relaxes me like the smell of fresh mown grass and the loud, grating sound of a lawn mower engine. It would give me time to think, to mull over the events of the last day.

As I paced the length of my yard repeatedly, the thoughts raced back and forth in my mind like hyperactive children wired on Halloween candy. What would I tell Christine? Should I tell her? If I did, she wouldn't let me hang out with the guys for a long, long time. I guess I just answered my own question. Although she assumed the guys and I were idiots, she didn't really want to know the details—so why should this be any different? Next question—why would anyone be trying to kill us? Am I in danger at home? Is my family? Is this about the four of us guys, or just aimed at Dave? *Well, this bites*, I thought. There were way too many questions for me to sort out while I cut the grass.

I puttered around the house, enjoying the chance to relax. I called Dave to see what they were up to and if anyone had tried to kill him in the last several hours. The answers were—"cleaning out the garage," and "very funny, Coop." Before I knew it, the kids returned from school and Christine came home from work. Shortly thereafter, I became immersed in helping with homework, catching up on the many important events that happened in elementary school in the last two days, and cleaning up from dinner.

I told Christine that Dave was doing okay, all things considered, and that he might decide to keep his dad's house. "He's going to keep it? Won't he be reminded of his dad all the time?" she asked.

"Nah, remember—it's the house he grew up in. It wasn't always just his dad's house. It'll be nice to have a place to hang out at in the old neighborhood," I replied. This proclamation was met with a look of scorn by Christine, which was intended to tell me that I wasn't going to be "hanging out with the guys" half as much as I would probably want to.

I adored Christine. By agreeing to marry me she had made my life complete, but she didn't understand the bond between my friends and me. She tolerated it, but she didn't understand it. She had her own opinions formed long ago that had been based on her first impression of them. In her mind, Dave was "the nice one," Cliff was "the womanizer" who thrived on regaling us with tales of his glory days, and Chuck was just our goofy little brother.

"Dad, come look at my drawing!" It was Michael, my youngest at eight. He was still at the age that parent's love was important, when he wants everything he does to be met with his parents' glowing approval. It was easy enough to give the reaction he wanted, since, as his dad, I thought everything he did was destined for greatness anyway. He was my kid—how could it not be?

"Wow Michael! I have never seen such an interesting picture! I love all the colors you used!" I had no idea what it was supposed to be, but he smiled and happily went back to his work.

"Dad, will you be able to go to my game on Saturday?" asked Nathan. He was my middle child, at ten years old. My little athlete. The apple of his dad's eye. He was named after one of my childhood friends. What dad didn't love having an athlete for a son? He had a basketball game on Saturday that I wouldn't miss even if my life depended on it. Hopefully it wouldn't, because that would really suck.

"Nate, I would give up my left arm before I missed a game of yours!"

"Very funny Dad, you're right handed anyway!" He didn't think I was as funny as I did. That's the fate of every dad I suppose. We're never recognized as the brilliant comedians we like to think we are.

"Of course I'll be there," I added. "If I don't go—who's going to yell at the refs?" He smiled and went back outside to practice.

"Hey, Dad, you got my allowance?" Ryan, my oldest, was starting to take on a bit of a surly attitude. At thirteen, he was starting to get the crazy idea that his parents weren't the coolest people in the world and that sometimes, he might even know more than us. He also seemed to be growing his hair to match his attitude. He was growing it out into that shaggy "skater" look that was popular with kids who wanted to look like outsiders.

Of course I had his allowance, but I wasn't going to give it up too easily. "So did you get your Global Studies report back?"

With a sigh and a look of scorn he obviously learned from his mother, "Yeah, I got a B on it—can I have my allowance now?" I was not to be deterred. From working with kids I knew he was behaving almost exactly as every other teenager in the world, but I didn't have to be happy about it.

I was hoping we could be different. I thought that by using all my professional knowledge and experience I would be able to have a happy, honest, and respectful relationship with my teenager. I was a moron in this regard. "So Ryan, is your girlfriend going on the class trip to Boston too?" He realized he was going to have to play ball a little if he wanted his money.

"Dad, she's not my girlfriend. Can't a girl who's my friend call me without you having to know every detail? Can I have my allowance now?" I forked over the money, although I wasn't sure why. I guess I was paying him to keep the lines of communication open, such as they were. I hated that he wasn't still that wide-eyed little boy that believed his dad just might be Spider-Man.

That night as I sat in bed taking notes for what I hoped would be my next book, I should have been relaxed. I was surrounded by my family. My human security blanket. Christine lay next to me watching TV, but quickly losing the battle to keep her eyes open. The problem was that I wasn't relaxed. The chaos of last night was still replaying over and over in my brain. My mind was still racing, trying to figure out what the hell had happened over at Dave's house. Everything Chuck said made sense, but still—it didn't make sense. It sure looked like someone had tried to kill one or all of us, but why? As far as I knew none of us had ever done anything bad enough that someone would want us dead.

The more I thought, the more I realized that there were some more pieces to this puzzle that I had forgotten about. The ticket. Why the hell had Gooby's dad been sneaking off to Tupper Lake? Were those mystery trips related to why someone was trying to kill Gooby, or all of us? No one could possibly know we had found the ticket. If no one could know, then why had someone tried to kill us? Were they trying to prevent us from going through his stuff? Who were "they"? I made a mental note to talk to Gooby about the ticket in the morning. I couldn't figure this all out tonight and I was getting tired. In an effort to unwind, I went back to my book notes. My publisher was counting on a third book by the end of June, in time to release it for the holiday season. Nothing says "Merry Christmas! I love you!" like a self-help book. After the loss of sleep last night, it didn't take long for my eyelids to grow unbearably heavy. Sometimes even my own work bored me to sleep. I set my notebook on the nightstand and snuggled up to my already snoozing Christine. *I'm home,* I thought as I drifted off to sleep.

Suddenly I felt a tapping on my shoulder. I wasn't sure how long I had been asleep. It was probably Michael, awakened from a bad dream. As I rolled over and looked up, I saw a tall, dark shadow looming over me. "Cooper, wake up. We have to talk." It was my father. I couldn't understand why he was in my house in the middle of the night. "Shhh. Follow me downstairs. I don't have much time," he said. Fortunately, Christine hadn't awoken. Something like this would totally freak her out. I followed him down the stairs. I didn't turn on any lights for fear of waking one of the kids. We stood at the back of the kitchen, as far from the stairs as possible. The ticking of that stupid owl clock Christine loved so much sounded as loud as a hammer pounding in the silence of the night.

"Dad, what are you doing? This is crazy!" I was trying to whisper, but my tension made it hard to keep my voice low.

"Shhh. Cooper, you need to listen. You and your friends need to be careful. There's more to these people than you realize. It's in the shed. Go there." He turned towards the back door and started to open it.

"Dad, wait, I need to know more!" Through the darkness I could see him looking me in the eyes. I felt goose bumps rise on my skin. I could feel his cold breath on my face as he spoke.

"I love you Cooper. I have to go."

I started to speak, but the only sound that came out of my mouth was a loud buzzing sound. The alarm. I always set my alarm clock. I did my best writing in the morning when the house was quiet. They say that your brain works on unsolved problems you have while you sleep. In fact I've read that if you've lost something, and you go to sleep thinking about it, you'll usually know where to find it when you wake up. I think that's what my brain had done in the form of a dream. My father. He and Gooby's dad had been friends since before we were born. He might know something.

6

Denial. The word was there. I picked up my notepad and stared at the small word scrawled on the bottom corner of the page. I just stared at it, dumbfounded. I could feel the apprehension rising within me. Denial. How did it get there? What did it mean? I had left my notepad on the nightstand. I could feel the blood draining from my face as the black letters stared up at me. Denial. The writing wasn't my own, nor did it belong to anyone in my family. I looked around the room. Everything else appeared to be normal. No broken windows, not a knick-knack out of place.

I pulled on my slippers and grabbed the notebook as I headed downstairs. I checked on the kids first. They were all still snug in their beds and breathing. The doors were still as locked as I had left them before I turned in for the night. I looked at the notepad again. Denial. Yup, it was still there. Damn. "What the fuck is going on?" I mumbled aloud to myself. Either I had written this in my sleep or someone had been in my house, literally standing right next to me while I slept.

A short while later, it took all of my Oscar-worthy acting talents to behave normally as my family woke and prepared for their day. I had taken the week off for the funeral and I was thankful I still had two more days off plus the weekend. As soon as everyone was out of the house I called Goob. One ring, two rings, three rings. As the rings seemed to go on and on, I started to fear the worst. *C'mon you idiots, pick up*, I thought to myself.

The sleepy voice of Chuck picked up a moment later. He reported that Dave wasn't up yet, but that nothing unusual had happened to them. I told him about the note.

His initial reaction was what I expected. "See? I told you someone is fucking with us! You didn't believe me, did you?"

I let Chuck enjoy his "told you so" for a moment before I said, "What do we do now?"

My first plan was to have a security system installed in my home. Christine and I had talked about this before, so it would be pretty simple to tell her that with my time off I had decided to get it done this week. Chuck knew a security company that did contract work for the government and with his connections he could get the work done today. The expense wasn't a problem. It was my family they were fucking with now, and I was pissed.

Chuck was a miracle worker as far as I was concerned. The system was in by two o'clock and I headed over to Gooby's house as fast as I could. For a change the guys hadn't been drinking yet, but were still sitting around in their boxers. I immediately showed them my notebook. They weren't as freaked as I was, but they hadn't had someone in their house while they slept. Chuck looked over my notes. "This is what you're writing about? You're no Dr. Phil." Chuck was lucky I didn't have his gun in my hand at that moment. I hated that freaking Dr. Phil.

They had completed a search of the basement before I got there, or so they said. We went back to the computer desk and searched every nook and cranny. Nothing else interesting turned up. Goob went to work searching his father's computer and flash drives for any files that might give us a clue. Colt, Gooby's dad, must have had about six of those little memory sticks at two GB each. *This was going to take forever*, I thought. I forgot about Dave's computer expertise. He was quickly able to instruct the computer to search its hard drive and each memory stick in turn for several key words and phrases. Tupper Lake and Shaheen's Motel were our first choices. Maybe the ticket didn't mean anything, but maybe it did. At my urging he added the word 'denial' to the search.

Chuck and I headed upstairs to the rooms. Every drawer and closet shelf was searched for anything unusual. Today there was a lot less of the usual inane and witless repartee that usually marked our days together. Chuck, being a bit more clandestine than I, showed me some of the tricks of the trade, such as feeling the seams and linings of clothing for anything sewn in. We went through the same routine with the pillows and bedding. We flipped the mattresses to look for any openings underneath or between where something might have been concealed. We knew we were looking for needles in the proverbial haystack, but what choice did we have? Something was going on and it looked like it could cost us our lives if we didn't figure it out.

"Hey guys! Come here!" Dave hollered from downstairs. Chuck and I raced like two stupid kids fighting to get the front seat of the car, trying to push and shove our way past each other all the way down the stairs. He may have been spy guy, but I still beat him there, laughing as I ran into the den where Dave sat at the computer. There it was. On the monitor in front of him in a little Windows box titled FLASHDRIVE (J:). One folder simply named: Denial.

We all just stared at it. It seemed as if no one even breathed for at least a minute, although it had to be much shorter. "Did you open it? " I asked.

"Nah, I couldn't. It's password protected," Dave said.

"There's got to be a way in, even without the password, isn't there?" asked Chuck.

Dave pulled the memory stick out of the front of the computer and held it up, looking at it thoughtfully. "I don't know. I'm going to have to think about this. If only I had all the software I have at work." At that moment the doorbell rang, startling us out of our thoughts.

I walked over to answer it. It was a little kid, no more than seven. He looked as if he had been in a fight. His face was swollen and bruised with a trickle of blood starting to dribble from his lip. His right hand looked like it had been through a meat grinder. "Can you help me, mister? I was skateboarding and I wiped out real bad. C-c-can I use your phone to call my m-mom?" He burst into tears. Damn that Tony Hawk.

We led him into the office and sat him down. Dave went to get a washcloth and some Band-Aids from the closet in the kitchen while I got him the phone. The boy was able to dial his number and reached his mom. Dave took the phone and gave her the house number. The boy only lived about eight houses away, but he must have been too hurt or scared to try to get himself home. He said his name was Joshua. By the time his mom arrived a few minutes later, we had also put together an ice pack for his lip. Chuck almost immediately snapped to military attention when he answered the door. Much to our pleasant surprise, his mother was none other than our new friend, Maria, from the other night. She still looked as attractive as our first impression of her.

As she checked out Joshua and saw that he wasn't as badly hurt as he first appeared to be, she turned to us and said, "I guess you boys weren't kidding when you said you look out for the neighborhood. Thank you. He never should have been this far from the house by himself." Dave offered Joshua some cold water as his mother tended to him. "How long have you lived here?" she asked Dave. He told her about his dad passing away and his plan to move into this, his old childhood home. "Well, I just want to thank you guys again for taking care of Joshua. It's a good thing you were home. I hope I see more of you around the neighborhood," she said with a hint of a smile. I could tell that both Chuck and Goob were savoring her last sentence in their minds.

I had a thought, a question that had been scratching at my brain like a piece of popcorn kernel that gets stuck between your teeth. It had been bothering me since yesterday. "Maria, before you go, I was just wondering—if your parents have lived in this neighborhood so long, how come we never saw you before?"

She hesitated and I thought I saw a glimmer of uncertainty in her dark brown eyes. "My parents were never big fans of the public schools, so they sent me to boarding schools my whole life. I spent summers with my grandmother up North. "Well, I'd better get my little guy home. He looks like he could use a nap." We said goodbye and she headed down the sidewalk with Joshua by her side.

"Man, there's nothing hotter than a good looking soccer mom," Goob said. Chuck and I burst out laughing. For some reason, ever since his divorce, Dave had a thing for soccer moms. I suppose it was because he had wanted his wife to become a soccer mom and now he was pining for what was missing in his life, a wife and son. My friends hated when I played psychologist on them, so I didn't voice this last thought, or the next. This Maria chick could either be very good, or very bad for Gooby. The problem was Chuck had dibs.

<h1 style="text-align:center">7</h1>

My parents had divorced when I was a teen. I held no grudges toward either one and still had relationships with both. Notice I didn't say "good" relationships. I learned when I was young to try to protect myself by not getting too involved in their ups and downs. Don't get me wrong, I still cared about them, but I never completely got over that habit of not expecting too much from them. That's why I was so surprised by my father's phone call right then. "Why hello, Cooper! How are you?" He never called me.

In my shock I nearly stammered my reply, "Hi Dad, I was going to call you today. I didn't even know you had my cell number." He apparently had gotten it from my sister. (Mental note: Tell sister to stop giving out my cell number.) He always seemed ill at ease talking to me, but today he seemed especially out of sorts as he explained that he needed me to come over to sign some paperwork so he could name me executor of his will. Apparently the death of Dave's dad, his longtime friend, had made him decide he needed to get his affairs organized. He was in good health as far as I knew, but I could understand why this was important to him right now. I was preparing to leave Dave's for the day anyway, so I asked if he minded if I stopped by in a few minutes on my way home.

"Of course not, oh, and I've got a bucket of balls for you." I think that was his way of bonding with me, giving me golf balls he collected from his walks along the course near his house. Hey, with a dozen good golf balls running about twenty bucks, who was I to complain?

My parents had sold our house and moved from the old neighborhood after the divorce. Although I stayed with both through summers and college vacations, it never felt like I lived at either place. I think I still liked to visit Gooby at his father's house just so I had a sense of home again.

I pulled into my dad's driveway a short while later. It was an almost rural area with homes few and far between along County Route 31. As I stepped out of the car, I noticed dark, swollen clouds gathering in the west and a breeze beginning to stir the treetops. It was going to storm soon. Even though my dad had lived here for the last eighteen years, it still seemed like I was visiting him in the wrong place. I don't think anyone ever really forgets their childhood home. Dad's "new" house was bigger in square footage than my childhood home, but somehow it always seemed sterile and empty because no one I knew had lived their life there.

I walked up the precisely constructed wooden steps and stood on the small deck he had built as a front porch. He still loved to build and stain things. I swear that if he could have built a car out of wood and stained it lightly to show the wood grain he would have done so. His whole family was like that. They were almost Amish. They actually gathered on weekends to build houses for each other occasionally. As a child I felt like an indentured servant, forced to help with his woodworking projects every weekend. The smell of sawdust still gives me flashbacks.

Although I certainly had permission to walk into his house, I knocked as I opened the door and walked in. "Dad? I'm here!" Hmm, no answer. I hope he hasn't passed out for his afternoon nap. I walked through the foyer. No one in the den to my right. He had left his computer on. At my last visit I had to help him figure out how to e-mail. He was always one for gadgets, but for some reason I never could figure out, he was always reluctant to join the internet fad. I'm sure he thought it was a fad that would pass eventually.

"Dad?" I walked into the kitchen. Still no answer. I was starting to get nervous. The counter only had a few empty Genesee Cream Ale cans, so he was probably still sober at this point in the day. I caught myself feeling judgmental, and pretty stupid based on my own drinking habits lately. He was retired. Why couldn't he have a cold beer during the day if he wanted one? The door to the basement stairs was open. I breathed a sigh of relief. He must be downstairs in his workshop and didn't hear me.

A shaft of light cut diagonally across the bottom of the stairs, but I didn't hear any power tools running. "Dad?" I called down. No answer again. I started down the stairs, afraid to go down, but afraid not to. The feeling that I was sneaking up on someone was made worse when I accidentally knocked a paint can off of the side shelf with my elbow and lunged crazily to catch it. I didn't make the catch and the can thumped down the stairs, echoing noisily as it rolled off to one side when it hit the bottom. The house again fell silent. If anyone else were here that sure as hell would have gotten their attention. I suddenly realized that the events of the last two days had totally rattled me. Here I was creeping down the stairs, terrified, in my own father's house, when he was probably just out in the back yard rummaging around his shed.

He wasn't in the shed. When I rounded the corner at the bottom of the stairs I saw him, and I ran back up the stairs and immediately threw up in the kitchen sink. My head felt as if it was spinning as I wiped the spittle from my mouth and nose with the towel left on the counter. I was dizzy and almost disoriented, gasping for breath. Suddenly I heard, *Should I stay or should I go now? If I go there will be trouble, if I stay it will be double.* I loved the Clash, but not right now. *My fucking cell phone is ringing,* I thought. It was Gooby so, in spite of everything, I answered.

"Coop, did you take the flash drive? We can't find it."

I coughed out the last bit of vomit and bile from my mouth. "Goob, get over to my dad's house. I need help." I flipped the phone shut and turned to lean against the kitchen counter. My knees buckled and I slid down to a sitting position. I rested my spinning head on my knees. My mind was reeling. I'm not sure how long I had been sitting there when I heard Goob's voice from the front door.

"Coop?" He walked in quickly, coming straight to the kitchen. Chuck and Cliff were right behind him. "What's wrong?" I just pointed to the door of the basement.

They came back a few minutes later, visibly pale. He was dead. The circular blade from his radial arm saw had somehow come loose and struck him in the neck. There was a lot of blood, but that wasn't the sole reason that Cliff, Chuck, and Dave appeared so pale. I hadn't noticed it in my shock and haste to flee from the horror I had discovered. Next to my father's outstretched hand, written in the blood and sawdust surrounding him, looking more like a grotesque finger-painting project, was one word. Denial.

The police and crime scene investigators concluded that no crime had occurred, just a tragic accident. An old, electric saw came apart after many years of use. The blade, still spinning at full speed when the bolt broke, had hit the table and literally taken off, hitting my father in the neck. Thankfully, his death had been almost instantaneous. The only puzzle for the police was why he had written the word "denial" as his last dying breath had left his body. The forensics expert determined that it had been written with his own hand, but what they said next hit me with the force of a blow to my stomach, taking my breath away.

"Well, Mr. Scott, judging from the color of the blood and how dry it is, combined with the condition of the body, I would estimate that your father's accident occurred between nine and eleven p.m. last night. When was the last time you spoke with him?"

I felt dizzy again. I reached out to steady myself on the kitchen table. I began to see gold flecks at the edges of my vision. The room spun and the gold flecks filled in my sight until only tunnel vision was left. Then it was gone too. *I hope someone catches me,* I thought as I lost consciousness.

I awoke, taking in deep breaths, surrounded by my friends. "Don't get up. Just lie there," Chuck said. We never listened to Chuck, so I pulled myself up to sitting, my back against the cupboard. Dave handed me a glass of cold water. I nodded and drank it all in huge gulps. I would love to say that I faked fainting just to avoid answering the coroners' question, but that would be a lie. Fortunately, my momentary loss of composure had the same effect. The police and forensics guys had gone to work doing their jobs while I had taken a brief respite from reality. I was conscious again now and reality still sucked.

Chuck, or *Spy Guy*, as we were quickly beginning to think of him, leaned in and whispered to the three of us. My breath still smelled like puke, but came closer anyway. "Ok, guys, we know without a doubt something is going on here, but so far everything has looked like an accident. The cops are too stupid to see anything but the facts as they are. We know differently. I think it's in our best interest to just shut our mouths about what we think and figure it out without the cops. If we rely on them, we'll all be dead within a week." We all nodded. I was still in shock and unable to do anything else. Besides, who was I going to trust—my friends of thirty years, or some cop who was only qualified to give out speeding tickets? Anyway, who were we to argue with *Spy Guy*?

Chuck and Dave took me back to Dave's house, while Cliff stayed back to lock up my father's house after the police and coroner finished up. Cliff was also going to start poking around; looking for any evidence that could give us an idea of where to go next. He was as motivated as any of us. His father was still alive, for now. Cliff was also kind enough to notify my sister, who, on paper, was still the executor of my father's will. She agreed to begin making the necessary arrangements for the second unexpected funeral in a week. My heart was still racing and I couldn't stop breathing as if I had just run a marathon. Gooby offered me a beer to calm my nerves. A beer definitely wouldn't do. I asked for a whiskey, straight up. Goob, never at a loss for alcohol, had a glass of Jack Daniel's ready for me momentarily. I took it all in one greedy swig. The burning sensation flowing down my throat actually seemed to clear my head.

8

Cliff

Cliff watched as the wheeled legs of the gurney automatically folded under as it was slid into the county coroner's van. The sky had grown dark and thunder had begun to rumble ominously in the distance. He let go of the curtains and turned around. He had never been in a dead guy's house by himself so soon after the death. *Shit, this is creepy. I wonder if ghosts really do exist,* he thought to himself. He decided that now was not the time he wanted to find out the answer to that question. Per Chuck's instructions, he headed to the computer first. The computer table was clean and empty of anything save a single pen in the top drawer. Cliff clicked on 'My Computer'. 'My Documents' was empty. There were no other files or folders. E-mail, inbox, sent, and deleted items were empty. Cliff went to the internet. The history had been cleared. The cookies folder was empty. Either Cooper's dad had just bought a brand new computer, or someone had thoroughly cleaned this computer of anything stored in its memory. *Hmm...cookies, I wonder if he's got anything good here to eat*, Cliff asked himself.

Cliff walked into the kitchen and looked around. It still smelled like Cooper's puke. *I can't eat with that smell*, he thought to himself. He opened a window to air out the room. "The rain hasn't started yet, that should be okay for a while," he muttered. He walked around opening cupboards and rummaging around. He opened the refrigerator and peered inside, hoping for something decently edible. What he saw was a lot of cheap beer, lots of condiments, a bottle of wine and *Yahtzee!* he thought. A package of ham, sliced cheese, and some rolls. "That'll hit the spot as long as the ham's not too old," he said aloud.

Suddenly he heard a knock at the door that made him jump. Even though he hadn't seen a ghost, he was still on edge. "Mr. Scott...?" came a tentative voice through the screen door. Cliff walked just as hesitantly to the front door. It was a boy, maybe eleven, looking as if he had just come from a Little League game, with his Yankees shirt and hat. Blond hair, blue eyes, and freckles. His eyes were an almost luminous blue, but one had an ugly bruise surrounding it, as if perhaps a he hadn't avoided an inside fastball in his last game.

That kid doesn't know what a Norman Rockwell painting is, Cliff thought, *but he sure as hell could star in one*. He reminded Cliff a bit of himself at that age. Cliff could see the boy's bike, with a baseball glove on the handlebar, laying on its side in the front yard. "Can I help you?" Cliff asked.

"Umm...I don't know. Is Mr. Scott home?"

Cliff couldn't think of a tactful way to explain, so he just said, "He's not here right now."

The boy paused, looking as if he were gathering his thoughts, deciding what to say next. He looked up at Cliff through the screen, looking him in the eyes. "I usually cut Mr. Scott's lawn, but his shed is locked—could you open it for me?"

Cliff let out a sigh. "I'm sorry kid, but you won't need to cut Mr. Scott's lawn anymore. He passed away today."

The boy turned and left without another word, practically sprinting to his bike. Cliff berated himself. *I shouldn't have just come out and said that. Damn it. That poor kid was just coming here to earn his baseball card money and I scared him like that. For all I know he may think I killed him. He's probably going home to call the police.*

As Cliff stared at the hedge where the boy had sped around the corner and disappeared from sight he felt a heavy drop of water hit his cheek, and then another. He looked up as the slow, heavy drops turned into a downpour that hissed on the driveway. A flash of lightning was followed quickly by a crack of thunder that caused him to literally jump backwards away from the door. "Damn, that storm must be almost on top of me," he said aloud.

Cliff walked quickly back to the kitchen to close the open window. The curtains were blowing in and a spray of rain droplets hit him in the face as he reached for the window. As he began to pull down, he thought he saw movement out of the corner of his eye. Through the downpour, Cliff saw that the shed door had blown open and was slamming against the wall. This was no average lawnmower and garden tools backyard shed. It was shaped like a small barn and built like a fortress. It loomed in the back corner of the spacious yard. "Oh fuck," Cliff muttered. "I thought that stupid kid said the shed was locked." Cliff thought to himself, *This is the part in every creepy movie when you sit in the theater screaming, 'Don't go in there!' but the dope always does anyway. I'm not going to be that dope.*

Cliff closed the window and finally made that kick ass ham and Swiss sandwich he had planned on. The rolls seemed a little stiff, but there didn't appear to be any mold on them so he forged ahead. The rain was hitting the windows in sheets, but that didn't change the taste of a good sandwich. Cliff prided himself on his ability to maintain his appetite regardless of the circumstances, and eating in a house shortly after a dead body was removed definitely topped his list of eating accomplishments. If it weren't Cooper's dad who just died, Cooper would appreciate the challenge of eating in this situation. *Mental note: After Coop is over his dad's death, tell him about this.* The only thing that equaled Cooper's passionate hatred of death was his passionate love of eating. It was perhaps why Cooper and Cliff liked going over to Gooby's so much. *WHAM!* (No, not the George Michael/Andrew Ridgley '80s glam pairing) *WHAM! WHAM!*

The slamming of the blowing shed door startled Cliff from his revelry. *Damn*, he thought. *I'm going to have to go out there and close that damn thing anyway.* He shoved another bite of his sandwich into his mouth, followed by a swig of beer and headed for the back door that opened off the kitchen onto— a magnificently constructed wooden deck. As Cliff tossed a patio chair that had blown over aside, he felt a sting and then another on his face as if someone was throwing tiny pebbles at him. The rain was coming down in sheets now and he was soaked to the skin almost immediately. His first thought was that the Norman Rockwell kid had come back to throw stones at him in the rain. That didn't make sense. The stinging on his face seemed to be increasing and whatever was hitting him felt like it was getting bigger. As he looked down he saw little, white pebbles bouncing off the deck at his feet. *Hail*, he thought. *This just keeps getting better and better.* He walked across the back yard, trying to shield his eyes from the hail, noting with disgust that his shoes were starting to make that squishy sound with each step as they became soaked with water. God he hated that. Why the hell had the guys left him here? Chuck was the big spy expert—why wasn't he here searching for clues?

Cliff reached the shed and corralled the swinging door. As he prepared to close and latch it, a little girl's voice issued from within. "Can you help me?" He could barely make out a small, dirt-streaked face in the back corner, as if the child was sitting, almost hiding in the darkness. He stepped forward into the shed. The mixed smells of dirt, gasoline, and grass clippings flooded his senses. He heard the slight shuffle of a foot on the dirty, wooden floor behind him and to the left.

As he began to turn, something slammed into his skull. Lights and blackness seemed to explode simultaneously in his vision as he fell forward. When he hit the floor, Cliff felt a sickening crack in his nose. He rolled over, trying to clear his blurred vision. He could make out a shadow moving towards him. He rolled onto his side, feeling cold metal beneath his face. He reached to feel it, grabbed whatever it was, and swung as hard as he could in the direction of the looming shadow. Cliff felt the metal object connect and registered a satisfying crunch as his unknown assailant fell to his knees.

As Cliff lay prone on his back, exhausted from the effort it took to defend himself, he could see a glint of metal as the blurry shadow raised something above his head. Cliff heard a whoosh and rolled to his right. A shot of pain momentarily cleared his vision as his broken nose grazed the floor. There was a thunk as a shovel stabbed into the wooden floor inches behind his head. Cliff swung the metal crowbar he had picked up, striking the shadow in the largest, darkest area. He hoped he had broken a few ribs. He heard the dark, blurry shadow gasping for breath. It sounded like the rough, coarse breathing of a very large man. The dirty-faced girl rushed past the two fallen men and out into the storm. Cliff could feel the rain blowing in on his face as thunder rolled across the sky overhead. The open shed door continued to blow and slam against the side of the shed. Cliff crawled towards his attacker, barely seeing, hoping to inflict more damage. A kick to his head ended that hope as the now very solid shadow pulled itself to its feet and limped out of the shed and into the gray, wet day.

Cliff lay on his back exhaling, unintentionally blowing a bubble through the flow of hot, sticky blood pouring from his swollen nose. His head began to swim as everything around him began to sway and spin. He closed his eyes. *I'll just rest for a minute*, he thought. As Cliff passed into unconsciousness his cell phone went off. *She was a fast machine, she kept her motor clean. She was the best damn woman I had ever seen…*

9

Gooby, Chuck and I sat around the kitchen table, each with a drink in our hands. The sound of rain outside was droning in the background. "You know, I've been thinking," Chuck said. "If we're going to be fighting someone or something that has now killed two or maybe three of our parents, do you think maybe we should cut back on our drinking?"

Gooby replied, "Dude, you may be nerves-of-steel *Spy*

Guy, but I'm not. I need a little something to help me wrap my brain around the idea that someone is trying to kill me for some reason I don't even know. Besides, it's not like it's eight o'clock in the morning right now. Normally we might be getting home from work about now and cracking open a beer anyway."

Gooby still said things like "dude" and "off the hook." I think he wanted to pretend he was younger than he was. In my opinion, once you're over thirty, it's time to throw out the slang handbook you purchased as a teen and start using all that vocabulary we had to learn for the S.A.T. My head was clearer now thanks to the whiskey and a little bit of time.

"I'm with Gooby," I added. "This is all getting a little too nuts for me, and I work with crazy stuff every day. Chuck, even though you deal with cloak and dagger stuff all the time—isn't it freaking you out that maybe whoever did this also killed your dad?"

"That's exactly why I'm so focused on this," he answered. "I want to get these fuckers as much as I've ever wanted anything."

Gooby suddenly spoke up with a different tone. "I wonder what Cliff is doing. We haven't heard from him and it's been over an hour since we left. I wonder if he's found anything."

"Why don't you call him?" Chuck suggested.

Our call went unanswered. We all knew that if Cliff didn't answer his cell he must be dead. He was so wired with 21st century gadgets that he probably gave off radiation that was picked up by satellites. A video camera cell phone that allowed him to check his e-mail and sports scores was just the beginning. If anyone was going to turn into a cell-phone zombie like the people in that Stephen King book, Cliff would definitely be first in line. His car talked to him, gave directions, and did everything but service him sexually. His tablet touchscreen computer and PDA were so ever-present that we began to wonder if he took them in the shower with him. I'm not sure his wife would even recognize him if he ever took that Bluetooth off the side of his head. If medical science gave Cliff the option of becoming a cyborg with all his electronic toys built into his body, I'm pretty sure he would jump at the chance. He hadn't answered his cell. That was definitely not a good sign.

We rushed out into the downpour and headed back to my dad's house. The gutters were overflowing from the deluge, covering the low-lying streets with standing water. Fans of water rose in our wake as Chuck took every turn without even considering the brakes. "Be careful you don't hydroplane," Gooby warned.

"Fuck hydroplaning," Chuck fired back. "If the tires touch the road it might slow us down." Chuck allowed himself a small, smug smile at this little bit of bravado.

As he kept his eyes on the road, Gooby and I briefly looked at each other and rolled our eyes as if to say, *Suddenly our little Chuck thinks he's all that.* (*Mental note: When things slow down later, make fun of Chuck so he doesn't get too cocky.*)

Although harrowing at times, we survived the ride out to my dad's house. Damn, I've got to stop thinking that. I don't have a dad anymore. The gravel driveway crunched under the tires as I arrived here for the second time today.

The house looked the same as always, but it felt different, and I didn't think I could walk in again yet. "You guys go inside. I'll check out back and in the shed."

Gooby and Chuck agreed easily enough. I think they understood exactly why I suggested it. Ever since that dream last night I'd been meaning to mention the shed to the guys. Had it been a dream, or did the ghost of my dead father visit me in the night? The second option was just too weird to believe, but why had I had a dream in which my father said something about the shed? What did he say exactly? The passing of daylight hours had robbed me of my memory of the details, but I remembered he mentioned the shed. That damn shed. As a fifteen-year-old he had stuck me out there on a cold, October day to dig the post-holes for it while he sat inside drawing up plans and cutting wood. I was still resentful of my weekends of indentured servitude. He died today and that was my first memory of my youth? *I must be a real asshole*, I thought. *To still be complaining about weekends of work with my dad.* There's nothing better to make you feel like a jerk than thinking bad thoughts about the recently deceased.

I slammed the car door shut, my face cringing at the feel of the wind-whipped rain hitting me. As I started across the lawn towards the corner of the house, I could hear Chuck and Goob's shouts of "Cliff! Cliff, where are you?" as they entered the house. I had already made one sickening discovery inside that house today—I wasn't ready to make another.

I rounded the corner and through the gray sheets of rain I could make out the monolith of a "shed" at the back corner of the yard. The door was swinging open and banging against the side. It wasn't like that when I left. I wonder who opened it. As I made my way across the yard and the door swung open again, I could make out something on the floor just inside the doorway. I hoped it wasn't what I looked like. I broke into a run. Unfortunately I slipped in the wet, muddy yard, going down hard into one of the filthy puddles.

Inside the house Gooby and Chuck raced from room to room, calling out Cliff's name. They again hesitantly ventured into the basement, fearful of another gruesome scene, but this time they were relieved to find it as clean as the coroner and police had left it.

As I got closer, I could make out the shape of a blonde head in the doorway. The door from the kitchen to the deck seemed to burst open as Chuck and Gooby virtually leapt out onto the deck. Chuck even went so far as to vault over the deck railing as he reached me and the shed two steps ahead of Goob. It looked bad. Cliff was lying prone on his back, his head in puddle of blood, and there was dark, wet, blood flowing from his nose, forming a goatee on his face. His chest however, was expanding and relaxing slowly. He was breathing.

I knelt and pressed two fingers to his neck. His pulse was slow and steady. "Don't move him for a minute," I said. "Cliff?" I repeated again, a little more urgently this time. "Cliff?" His green eyes slowly opened, but they looked glassy and unfocused. "Hold still for a second," I said. I covered his eyes with my hand for a moment and then pulled it away quickly. His pupils dilated. That was good.

Chuck jumped in, "Can you speak?"

Cliff replied in a gravelly voice, "I can, but why the hell would I tawg to you?" We looked at each other and smiled.

Cliff had a broken nose and, in all likelihood, a mild concussion. I volunteered to take him to the emergency room while Chuck and Gooby resumed searching my dad's house. We helped Cliff to Chuck's car and I headed to University Hospital.

Like almost every emergency room in the country it was busy and it looked like we were in for a long wait. There was the obligatory kid with what was probably a broken arm over there, the standard construction worker with the lacerated hand on the other side of the waiting room, the mom with the crying infant pleading with the triage nurse at the desk, your average talking-to-himself schizophrenic constantly circling the room, making everyone even more uncomfortable, and the domestic dispute stabbing victim being rushed past us all on the stretcher. "See that?" I said. "If you could have gotten yourself stabbed we'd be in there already."

"Thaks, I'll dry do remember thad nexth dime," he replied. The automatic doors to the outside seemed to be constantly open as new victims entered and others went out for a smoke. The cool breeze from the outside ushered in the smell of worms on the pavement. The dull roar of the constantly stirring milieu drowned out the sound of the one tiny television mounted on one of those metal arms sticking out of the wall.

Eventually Cliff and his now enormously swollen nose were taken back to his own little curtained room to await examination by the harried staff of the E.R. We followed the nurse past the desk with the large white board on the wall behind it. The white board seemed to cover the wall for at least twenty feet with names written top to bottom in marker destined to be wiped away and replaced the moment a room was vacated. The title "Emergency Room" is actually a misnomer at University Hospital. Unless you're a psychiatric patient requiring restraint, each "room" is nothing more than floor to ceiling curtains offering little to no privacy. The psych. patients got the really posh digs with rooms with walls and doors that locked from the outside.

Despite the fact that only Cliff's head needed an exam, (we all said this was far overdue), he had to strip to his boxers and put on one of those oh-so-attractive hospital gowns. Cliff was forced to sit on the bed while I was afforded a cozy, back-straightening plastic chair. I sure as hell wasn't in any danger of falling asleep in that torture device while we waited. The nurse's aide took vital signs, asked a few medical history questions, and then turned to me and said, "Are you his ahem...'friend'?"

I was about to answer the question when the light went on in my head. "Oh, am I his 'friend'?" I said, using finger quotes. Usually that just seems stupid, but in this case the finger quotes were exactly what the situation called for. "Why yes I am!" I practically bellowed. Cliff may have been concussed, but he wasn't past being embarrassed.

At the emergency room, or any doctor's office for that matter, getting your vital signs taken may seem like an act that gets you closer to being seen by an actual doctor, but I'm convinced that it's nothing more than something they do to placate us. In fact, I'm pretty sure they're just making those numbers up. Cliff was feeling a bit better thanks to a boatload of ibuprofen they had given him.

While we waited, we amused ourselves eavesdropping on the conversations of the hospital staff and other patients waiting in their curtained rooms.

From the "room" to our right we heard an exam beginning. The occupant was complaining more about his wait than his actual injuries. "When St. Bernard's Hospital was open, I never had to wait like this."

"That's exactly the problem," the doctor replied. "With St. Bernard's closed we don't have enough beds to meet the demand. You'll have to be patient. Now would you please tell me how you received these injuries?"

An exasperated sigh issued through the curtain. "Even when St. Bernard's was open, I got better service. I don't have to tell you anything. You just do your job."

10

As I not so patiently waited it out at the hospital with Cliff, Chuck and Goob began their search of my dad's house. "Well, where do we start?" Gooby asked.

"The basement," Chuck answered without hesitation. "He was found dead there. It's possible there's a reason for that." Their search of the basement, including opening every can of paint and jar of nails, turned up nothing except a stash of vintage Playboy magazines that dated back to the 1970s.

They moved to the upstairs of the house but their

efforts were similarly fruitless. Gooby drew the same conclusion that Cliff had. The computer had been cleaned—virtually all files in the memory had been deleted. "You know what, Chuck?" Gooby said. "There's one place we haven't looked. You know how you said that there might be a reason Coop's dad was found in the basement? There might also be a reason Cliff was attacked in the shed."

Suddenly from Gooby's hip came, *My blood runs cold. My memory has just been sold. My angel is the centerfold, angel is the centerfold.* He grabbed his cell. "Coop, what's up?" he answered. "Is Cliff going to survive? Alright, see you in a few." He turned to Chuck, "They're on their way. Let's hold off on the shed for now. You wanna grab a beer from the fridge?"

Our neighbors' impatience in the E.R. worked to our advantage, as the doctor was more than happy to conclude his business with him as quickly as possible. Cliff was seen next. He had already been sent for X-rays, which fortunately didn't show any skull fractures. The broken nose was quickly confirmed and taped up. By now it was ten-thirty at night. "You know, I was thinking," I said. "I'm starting to see a pattern in all the things that have happened over the past couple days. Let's get back to my dad's house. I want to see what Chuck and Goob think." After paying a small fortune to get out of the hospital parking garage we headed back to the scene of at least two crimes.

Despite state laws against using a cell phone while driving, I made a call to Christine. She wasn't happy. She was less happy when I told her that I wasn't coming straight home. Crazy as it may seem, she was under the impression that since my father had died today that I should be home with my family. If I told her all that had happened she'd kill me for not coming straight home. I gave her the Cliff Notes version, leaving out anything that might imply I could be in any danger. We had the security system. Everything should be fine at home.

Christine was pissed, but she knew from the beginning that "the guys" were part of my life. She didn't always like it, but she grudgingly accepted it during times like these. She couldn't understand it now, but I had to live with that until I could explain all this to her. With the assurance that I would explain everything to her eventually, I told her I'd be home by "(audible gulp)…one o'clock." I gave a quick, "I love you. I'll see you in a little while," and then hung up so fast that she didn't have time to squeeze in another word of protest. Man, was I screwed when I got home, and not in the good way either.

Sitting around the kitchen table at my dad's house I laid it all out for them, or at least as much as I could guess at. "Ok, now we have no doubts that something is going on. In fact, this is a war. A war we can't afford to lose. We need to come up with a plan. We can't just sit back and wait for whoever this is to pick us off one by one. So far, aside from Cliff's ass kicking, it's been our dad's they've killed, so what's the connection between them? Why would anyone want to kill them?"

Chuck spoke up first, "Before we go any further, everybody follow me."

We all sported the same slightly puzzled looks and all rolled our eyes behind Chuck's back as we followed him outside. He led us to his car and instructed us to get in. "C'mon Chuck," Gooby said. "Isn't this a bit much?"

"Just humor me please. Get in." As we sat in the car, Chuck resumed speaking, "Cliff, you know your dad is the only one who can answer these questions for us. Is it too late to call him?"

"Id's nod too lade," Cliff replied. "Bud he's nod home. He and hith wife are on vacation in Florida." We all paused, thinking.

"Shit," I said. "That's good and bad. With him gone we can't possibly question him, but at the same time, it probably keeps him safe. Cliff, I think you should at least call your dad and tell him what's going on. Chuck, can you help him get a secure phone line for that call?"

Chuck replied, "No problem. In fact, that's good thinking, Coop. You're on the right track. There are two things I can do for all of us. Based on the fact that whoever is doing this seems fairly adept at manipulating computers, we can assume that they're fairly technologically savvy, and not just with computers. To protect ourselves we're going to need a little bit of technology ourselves. I've got my tool kit in the trunk of my car. First, I'm going to equip each of our cell phones with voice encryption. It's just a little device we can snap into the data port of our phones, making it impossible for anyone to listen to or understand our cell phone conversations."

Cliff smirked and interrupted, "Ooh Thuck, id geds me tho hod when you tawg like a pie."

When our laughter subsided, Chuck replied, "I think Cliff's voice is already encrypted, but get ready for a cold shower anyway because you're going to love this next bit too. I'm going to let each of you borrow a bug detector. It will let us know if anyone is monitoring us anywhere we are."

Chuck drove us back to Gooby's house and gave us a quick lesson on how to operate the devices. We decided to practice using the bug detectors, ("yes, that's what they're really called" Chuck told us), to make sure Gooby's house was 'clean'. The other three of us completely loved this spy shit and we didn't think for a minute that Chuck wasn't enjoying showing off either. He had grown up a long time ago, but within the roles of our little group he was still the little brother that we picked on. The group scapegoat. Now he was getting a chance to show us that he was an actual adult. When this was all over, whatever 'this' was, Chuck would definitely deserve new respect from his longtime friends. He probably won't get it though. We're idiots when we're together.

We crept slowly around the house, not really expecting to find anything. Chuck was upstairs, Gooby on the main floor, and me in the basement. *It figures*, I thought. *I get the basement*. This was just like that time when I was twelve years old and home alone watching *Poltergeist* right before I had to go to bed in my basement bedroom. I was just as sure now as I was then that the boogeyman was about to jump out and grab me.

At first the only illumination was the light that filtered down the stairs and the dim, green glow of the display on my detector. I walked forward, arm outstretched, searching for the pull chain to turn on a light. It wasn't my house, so I didn't have that sixth sense of knowing where everything is when you're walking around in the dark. If someone wanted to kill me down here, I was screwed. My eyes hadn't adjusted to the darkness yet. Finally my hand found a chain in the dark and I cursed as I knocked it away from myself first before grabbing it as it swung back. I pulled and the dusty, old bulb on the ceiling provided enough light that I could finally exhale. It didn't look like I was going to be killed after all. The basement was one big room with the only hiding place being behind the furnace. I made a quick circle of the place with my detector remaining silent.

As I ascended the stairs I heard, "BEEP, BEEP, BEEEEEEEEEP!" I stormed up the steps, adrenalin flooding my senses. I practically leapt into the kitchen only to hear footsteps pounding overhead. Gooby's bug detector had gone off. The little indicator light on the front had switched over to steady red. He was in the dining room standing next to the table. "Hey Chuck," he shouted. "Come here. I've got something." Chuck almost literally flew down the stairs, taking two or three at a time. With a quick motion he immediately shushed us and grabbed Goob's bug detector, shutting it off. We all did the same with ours. We stood quietly and watched him search the room.

It only took a few moments for Chuck to locate the bug stuck to the back of a picture frame. He carefully lifted the sunset picture from the wall and carried it upstairs. Chuck carefully and quietly set it down in the small bedroom and tiptoed out, closing the door behind him. We returned to the dining room and resumed sweeping the house in silence. Chuck detected a tap on the phone but left it in place. After determining that there were no more bugs to worry about we returned to the dining room. By now, Chuck seemed very much in charge. "Ok, here's how I see this. They may know we're onto the fact that something is going on, but they don't know that we've found the bug and the phone tap. We can use that to our advantage. I'm not sure how, but just stay out of that one room and don't use the landline until we decide what to do with them.

Coop, you had another idea too, didn't you?"

I took a deep breath and began, "I may be imagining this, and I may be a little paranoid because of the combination of the circumstances and my work, but it can't hurt to be careful." I looked around the room and no one was smirking or looking to make a joke. I continued, "Watch out for kids."

Gooby looked incredulous. "What? Why?"

"Here's why," I replied. "Think about it. Over the last two days, every time something weird has happened to us there was always a kid nearby just before it happened." I paused, almost for dramatic effect, as I let my words sink in. I could see Cliff and Goob mulling this over. "Think about it." I said. "I work with kids every day. I notice them and what they're doing wherever I am. I don't know why, but I suppose I'm not very good at leaving my work at the office. Don't worry, I decided a long time ago that you guys are nuts."

Cliff looked like he was about to make some wiseass remark, then again, he always looked like that, but Chuck gave him a 'don't even think about it' look and he almost visibly bit his tongue. I continued, "Just before we were almost run over, I noticed a few goth-looking kids strolling through the neighborhood. Then remember when we found that flash drive at your dad's house, Goob? Who was there that afternoon before we discovered it was missing later?"

The light went on over Gooby's head. "Maria and her son! Yeah, but you can't think a little kid had anything to do with all of this, can you?"

I didn't want to seem overzealous, or like I was reading too much into things because of my work with child-cult victims, but this was starting to sound like something very bad was happening on a bigger scale than we initially thought. I continued without answering Goob's question. "Cliff, remember what you told me? First that kid came to the door wanting into the shed and then later the shed is open, you go out there and there's a kid inside just before you get the shit beat out of you."

"Hey!" Cliff interjected. "I didn't exactly get my ass kicked. I'm pretty sure I broke his leg and a rib or two!"

Chuck picked up where I left off, "You know what though, we don't know who those kids were or who that guy was over at Cooper's dad's house and I'll bet you anything the neighbors didn't see them today and probably wouldn't recognize them if they did. What we do know is where Maria and her kid live. One of us needs to start keeping tabs on her. She's our only connection right now."

Cliff, Goob, and I briefly made eye contact before we all burst out laughing. Cliff jumped in first. "You are pathetic, Chuck. You'll do anything to get laid, won't you?"

My brain, usually in tune with any opportunity for a joke, had been busy. "Hey you guys," I said, "I just realized something! Think about it. Every kid we've seen has also been hurt! Maria's kid was busted up from his skateboard 'accident.' Cliff, didn't you say the kid that came to the door had a black eye? What about the little girl in the shed? Did you get a good look at her?" I looked at Cliff as he thought.

"No, I didn't get a good look; I was too busy trying

to keep my head attached to the rest of me." As a professional who worked with kids that had been the victims of cults, I was starting to see a very disturbing pattern and I was more certain by the minute that I wasn't reading too much into this.

11

Cliff and I needed to go home. Despite everything that had happened in the last few days, we couldn't forget our families. Although we still acted like the adolescents we used to be when we were together, Cliff and I had to occasionally put on the adult suits we chose to wear when we started a family. With our usual group handshake and warnings to be careful, Cliff and I got in our cars and headed home. The pouring rain of earlier had abated, leaving a heavy fog that muted the glare of the streetlights. The roads were nearly deserted at this time of night. As I turned onto my street I looked at every house, wondering what secret might be lurking here, right in my own backyard. The events of the last few days had made me question the safety of everything in my little world. I pulled into my driveway. Everything looked okay, but I'd swear I saw the light go out in my thirteen-year-old son, Ryan's room as I pulled in. *Not a big deal*, I thought to myself. What teenager didn't stay up late on a school night watching a little extra TV or playing a game on his Xbox? As long as he passed everything in school, I was content not to fight him on every issue.

I went inside and headed straight for my bedroom. Christine had waited up, reading in bed. She looked ready to start an argument, but when I saw her I just collapsed with the grief of my father's death washing over me. I fell into her arms and just sobbed for what seemed like forever before I slowed and seemed to run out of tears. She began to kiss the tears on my cheeks and before I knew it, I was kissing back harder. I needed her and we made love. When we were worried and couldn't talk, it was how we reassured ourselves that everything was okay. It was a little immature to substitute physical intimacy for emotional intimacy, but it worked for us. Then again, isn't that what everyone does in spite of what their therapists tell them? I broke into tears a little while later as we lay in bed and she comforted me. After the weirdness of me not coming straight home after discovering my dead father, I think she was relieved that I was behaving somewhat normally. Finally my exhaustion caught up to me and my entire body suddenly felt too heavy to move. There were no dreams of my father coming to visit me. I closed my eyes and when I opened them again it was morning.

12

The light of the sun streamed through my window. The noises of my family getting ready for school and work filled the house.

"Mom, where's my lunch?"

"Mom, do you have a stapler for my report?"

"Hey! I called the shower first!"

"Don't forget to give that note to your teacher!"

God it was reassuring to be home and hear the

normal sounds.

Christine walked in and kissed me on the forehead. "How are you, honey? Are you sure you're going to be OK home by yourself today?"

I assured her that I was as well as I could be, and I'd be fine if she went to work. I was meeting my sister at the funeral home at nine o'clock to help with the arrangements and then it was back to my dad's house. My sister had no idea I had ulterior motives in my offer to go start cleaning out his house, but it was fine with her if I did the heavy lifting. This had to be the most bizarre week of my life. Two deaths and at least two attempts on my life. *Damn, I need needed a vacation.*

Of course, my first call was to Gooby and Chuck. They had survived the night without any more theatrics. After an hour at the funeral home, I headed straight over to Gooby's house. It was still technically his dad's house, but I was already back to thinking of it as 'Gooby's house'. His house was always the hangout when we were younger. He had the big pool in the summer and the snowmobiles in the winter. There was the rec room in the basement where we secretly hung out and got drunk as teens. As I said, as a group we are creatures of habit and when things got tough this week, it looked like we were falling back into old habits. In this case though, that might not be a bad thing. We needed to be in the old neighborhood to find out what was going on before it found us.

Although it was the truth, being there to clean out Gooby's house was as good a cover as any. Listen to me! Using words like 'cover'. If real people weren't getting really killed, playing spy like this would be totally awesome. Only now, instead of rubber-band guns and firecrackers, we had one real gun, voice encryption devices, and bug detectors. It was hard not to keep thinking, *We're idiots. What the hell do we think we're doing*? We trusted each other and we trusted Chuck. We've always done everything together and this was going to be no different. As I pulled into Goob's driveway, I was already thinking of how to present the rest of my ideas about this without sounding crazy. Last night I was too tired to give them all my theories, plus I think we all had enough to chew on as it was. As I had always done as a kid, I just walked into the house as if I lived there.

Goob and Chuck were sitting around in their boxers and t-shirts having coffee and watching Dr. Phil when Cliff and I arrived. (I hate that smug bastard Dr. Phil. He gets Oprah to lay off the carbs for a few weeks and he becomes a pop-culture icon. How fair is that?) I accepted the proffered cup of coffee and sat down on the couch. *Well, no point in beating around the bush*, I thought. "Goob," I said aloud. "You realize you're going to have to put the wood to Maria, right?" Cliff did a serious spit take, spraying his coffee all over my leg and the coffee table. "Shit, thanks, you bastard, "I said.

Gooby looked at me with that fake incredulous look he has, as if he hadn't already thought of this possibility. "What do you mean?" he stammered.

"I mean exactly what said," I replied. "It's pretty obvious that Maria and her kid may be involved. You basically live down the street from her now. You need to get in good with her and use that to find something out, and if that means getting jiggy with it, then you gotta do what you gotta do." I sat back and smirked as I took a sip of my coffee.

Of course, Chuck spoke up. "First of all, Coop,

please don't say 'jiggy' again, and secondly, you forget, I called dibs on Maria."

I burst out laughing, almost paying Chuck back for his spit take a minute ago. "Chuck, just because you're desperate to get laid," Gooby said, "it doesn't mean we all have to be stupid with you. Cooper is right. I can easily keep an eye on Maria without looking suspicious."

"Also," I interjected, "if she thinks she's playing you while you're playing her, that's even better. Just don't get yourself killed."

After Chuck and Goob got themselves dressed, Cliff and I headed over to my dad's house to finish our search. Chuck had to head to work for a little while. Goob had strict instructions to make himself very visible by working in the yard and possibly walking down the street if he saw Maria outside. Now it may sound simple for a good-looking man in his thirties to charm a single soccer mom, but this was Gooby we were talking about. I suppose I'm still influenced by memories of Gooby taking my sister to the prom all those years ago and not-so-suavely leaning on the doorbell Richie Cunningham-like as he prepared for his unsuccessful attempt at a goodnight kiss. Surely he had learned to relax and talk to women by now.

13
Gooby

Goob watched us pull out of the driveway and walked down to his mailbox by the street. *Well, I might as well get this started*, he thought. As he stood idly looking over the headlines in the morning paper he glanced up the street to see Maria, at least fifty yards away but clear as a bell, walking towards her mailbox. As Maria looked in his direction, Goob gave a wave he wasn't sure would be seen. His heart froze as Maria waved back and then, to his surprise, started walking down the sidewalk in his direction. He gulped and could feel his pulse begin to race. Gooby's breathing became audible and he noticed his palms were slightly sweaty as they held the paper. *Shit*, he thought. *What do I do now? This wasn't supposed to happen this fast or this easy. Ok, Dave, slow down, relax. She's just coming to say hi. No, wait, this is weird. Why would she...*

"Hi, Dave," Maria said as she walked up. She stopped just slightly inside his comfort zone, what people always call their 'personal space'. You don't know exactly how to measure it, but you know when someone has crossed that invisible line. Maria crossed that invisible line ever so slightly as she sidled up to talk to Gooby. Despite the fact that it was only about nine-thirty in the morning, she looked fully made up, but definitely not dressed for work. She wore a nicely fitting tank top with some yoga pants that left little to the imagination. At least to Gooby's fevered little imagination anyway.

"So what are you doing home during the week?" she said.

Gooby drew in a breath. "I'm still working on cleaning up my dad's stuff. There's not much more to do this week. Being here has brought back a lot of good memories. I'm thinking about moving back here. I could ask the same—what are you doing home today?"

Maria explained that she had taken the day off because she had some errands to run. Her parents were spending the weekend at her sisters in Ithaca, so she had to make the most of the free time to get things done. This was it. The opportunity was too good to pass up. Goob was about to ask Maria if she wanted to have lunch with him when she spoke first. "Hey, Dave, do you know anything about gas grills? Mine just quit on me the other day, but I've got a full tank of propane."

Shit, Goob thought. *What do I do?* He knew what he had to do. "Yeah, um, well, it could be a few things. You want me to come over and take a look?" If he could have said "Doh!" like Homer Simpson while hitting his head with a fist he would have. *Damn*, he thought. *Why do I have to sound like such an idiot?*

Maria smiled as she leaned in a little closer. She smelled nice. Her unwavering eye contact was a little unnerving this close, but her deep, glossy brown eyes were breathtaking. So were her lips. Gooby couldn't stop looking at them, among other things, as she spoke. "No, you don't have to come over right away," she said. "I have to go out for a little while. If you want to come over around noon, I can cook up some burgers on it after you fix it. How's that sound?"

"Um...ok." Way to go, Homer. Gooby stood at his mailbox, watching her as she walked away. If he was a cartoon character, his chin would be on the ground and his tongue rolled out. It was going to be hard not to get distracted.

14
Cooper

Gooby called us to tell us what he was going to be

doing. After a few jokes about the possibilities, we let him go back to working on his dad's house and Cliff and I went back to work at my dad's. Our first stop now was the shed. The kid had wanted in and Cliff had been assaulted when he went back there. It was possible that there was a reason for all that. My dad was dead, so there was no reason we couldn't empty the place completely and search every nook and cranny.

My dad had every imaginable large, motorized tool possible in that shed, or so it seemed. It took us an hour and a half just to empty the shed before we could even begin to examine the inside of the structure. We climbed into the loft, thinking that might be the most logical place to hide something since it was also the most difficult to get to. I lead Cliff up the ladder built into the wall. As a kid, this climb had been quick and easy. As an adult, the ladder seemed a little higher up and the opening at the top a little smaller. As I poked my head through the square hole into the loft, the old smells of must and mold triggered memories of hiding out here playing spy as kids, and when we were older, of sneaking up here to have a few beers that we filched from my father's refrigerator in the basement. The watery, bitter taste of cheap beer seemed so vivid that I thought I could taste it.

I heaved myself up through the hole, followed by Cliff, who seemed a bit more adept at climbing than I was. As our bodies blocked the hole, it was almost pitch-black. Remembering that this shed was where Cliff had gotten his head kicked in; I quickly switched on my flashlight. My first thought was also triggered by a memory. I did a quick sweep with my flashlight to check if there were any live hornet's nests tucked away in a rafter.

As I looked around the loft, I'd swear I had stepped

back in time. It didn't look any different than the last time I had been up here. I suppose it's possible that it hadn't been touched. As my father got older, he may have given up climbing into the loft altogether. I sure as hell know I'm probably only about ten years away from giving up on climbing things like this. I set my flashlight down on the old camping stove we had used when I was a kid and Cliff and I began our search.

The loft wasn't tall enough for us to stand in, but we could move around on our knees without bumping our heads. The dark, stuffy loft was filled with the smell of decaying canvas and probably more than one dead mouse. "How about we start at the far end," Cliff suggested. "You take that side and I'll take this one." I wished I had gloves. The old camping equipment was filled with dead bugs and the ancient canvas tent had rotted so badly that it fell apart in my hands. Despite the fact that I could kneel and move about comfortably, I apparently couldn't resist the urge to bang my head on a rafter a few times.

As we waded through the rotting remnants of my childhood, Cliff noticed that although the loft had smelled bad when we got up there, the smell had changed. "Oh no," I said with a chuckle. "You're not blaming this on me. I may be lactose intolerant, but I haven't had milk in years."

Cliff replied, "No, I smell gas. Real gas. Do you smell it?" After a pause to sniff the air, I admitted that I did smell gas. We hadn't knocked anything over, so the smell had to be coming from down below. Being closer to the opening to the ladder, I scampered over, looked down, and sniffed. The smell of gasoline was strong. Too strong.

I turned to tell Cliff that we had to get our asses out

of there, when I suddenly heard the shed door down below slam shut, momentarily blacking out the light coming up through the hole—but only for a moment. At the noise of the door slamming, Cliff scrambled to my end of the loft. Looking down, we suddenly saw a flickering orange glow and felt a wave of heat burst up through the hole. *Holy shit, we're fucked*, I thought. And then immediately after thinking it, I said it aloud. Yep, it sounded about right. The shed was on fire and we were trapped in the top of it with our only escape route blocked by flames. With the gas cans for the lawn mower down there, we might only have moment before there was an explosion.

15
Gooby

Gooby headed back into the house, finding it difficult to wipe the shit-eating grin off his face. Sure, she may have asked him over to her house just because she was part of a murderous cult, but what if she wasn't? What if she was genuinely interested in him? What then? *I'll tell you what then,* Gooby thought. *I'll finally get laid for the first time in two years. Screw Chuck and Coop and their plans. They can go play commando if they want to. We're not eleven anymore. I want sex with a partner for a change.*

That being said, if only to himself, Gooby headed into the house and began an extensive grooming and hygiene routine that would make someone with OCD say, "Are you sure that's not too much washing?"

As noon approached, he finished ironing his khaki shorts and Polo shirt and spritzed on a little body spray. Not once did it occur to him that he might seem a little foolish showing up to fix her gas grill with cologne on. Then again, considering that the goal was to get Maria to trust him whether she was a nutjob or not, it couldn't hurt to prepare for the best possible outcome.

After one more mirror check he finished getting dressed, being careful not to sit down and ruin the new crease he had made in his shorts. Then he grabbed his small toolbox and headed out the door. It was a beautiful, sunny day and he was walking down the street to have lunch with an attractive woman. It was a weekday and the neighborhood was exceptionally quiet. Not a car went by as Gooby walked the ten houses or so up the street. The combination of the sunshine and his elated mood made him think of that old Disney movie song, *Zip-A-Dee-Do-Dah, Zip-A-Dee-A*. He felt like skipping for a moment, but restrained himself. His next thought sobered him up a bit. *What if I can't fix her grill?*

As Gooby approached the quaintly decorated, yellow Cape Cod, Maria opened the front door and gave a friendly wave. Gone was the tracksuit from earlier this morning. Apparently they had both spent the morning getting 'all dolled up' as his parents used to say. Maria was in sandals, khaki shorts, and a sleeveless blouse, and she still smelled good. She held the door open and as he stepped inside, he noted that her toenails and fingernails sported a matching shade of pink polish. Gooby loved details like that.

"Hi Dave," she said with a warm smile. "I hope you don't mind this. I really appreciate you coming over."

Gooby replied, "No problem. I'm glad to have a break and glad to have the company."

"Where are your friends today?" Maria inquired.

"Oh they're at Cooper's dad's house. He passed away yesterday. Cliff is at work," Gooby answered. He watched Maria's face as he mentioned Cooper's dad.

After a moment's hesitation, she replied, "Oh my. That's terrible. What a week for you guys!" Was there a flicker of recognition, of knowing? Gooby wasn't sure.

"Well come on in," Maria said as she turned away. "Let me show you the grill."

Gooby followed her through the foyer and into the kitchen. He made a mental map of the house as he walked through. Dining room to the right, one set of stairs across from the front door, bedrooms upstairs, family room on the left, kitchen in the back. Exit to the garage on the far right side of the kitchen and sliding glass doors out onto a small patio that was surrounded by a privacy fence. He noted pictures of her son, Joshua, and a few of them together, on the walls, but no one else. If, as Maria said, she had recently moved back into this, her parents' home, it certainly didn't look like the home of an elderly couple. The decorating was tasteful and light. Bright beige, blue, and white colors that evoked thoughts of a seaside home were everywhere. The kitchen had gorgeous stainless-steel appliances that must have cost a small fortune very recently. He also noticed that Maria had a great ass at the top of her shapely, tanned legs as he followed her through the house. *I sure hope she's not part of an evil cult*, he thought to himself.

She opened the door to the patio and he followed her out. Gooby felt a wave of heat as he stepped out of the house. The midday sun, high in the sky, was baking the grooved, interlocking paving stones that made up the surface of her patio. The grill was off to the side by the six-foot-high slatted fence. "I'll be darned if I know what happened to it," Maria said. "It was working one day and the next it wasn't."

Gooby opened the light metal lid as if it were the hood of a car and looked inside. *She said 'darned,'* he thought. *If that isn't the cutest thing. Nobody in an evil, child-beating cult would say 'darned.' She's got to be good.* He hoped anyway.

After inspecting and tightening all the valves and hoses, Gooby decided to take a chance on lighting it. He hadn't really fixed anything, but what the hell? It couldn't hurt to try. Even though he had only been outside ten minutes, he was starting to sweat. Gooby graciously accepted the lighter and a cold beer from Maria. For a second he felt the heat of her skin as their fingers touched when she handed him the beer. Their eyes met and Maria didn't shy away from the eye contact or from the brief touch of Gooby's hand. "I'll be right back," she said. "I'm going to whip myself up a quick margarita."

He watched her walk away as she stepped inside and closed the sliding glass door behind her. Goob realized this whole visit would be a moot point either way if he couldn't get the grill working. He opened the valve from the propane tank and could hear the whisper of the gas beginning to flow into the grill. *I have no idea why she doesn't have a grill with an electric starter yet,* he thought to himself. *She's got a thousand-dollar refrigerator, but she can't get a grill made during this decade?*

He looked underneath, locating the small hole for the lighter. He poked the long nose of the grill lighter through the hole and triggered the flame. At first there was nothing, and then he was rewarded with the reassuring pop of the propane catching. He withdrew the lighter and looked inside. Sure enough, it was lit. As promised, Maria threw together a salad and quickly cooked up burgers for both of them on the grill. Because of the heat, they took their lunch inside and sat on barstools, eating at the island in the kitchen.

They talked about their childhoods and eventually how they found their way to this point in their lives. Maria was almost shockingly matter-of-fact as she discussed how Joshua's father, her last serious relationship, had abruptly disappeared after she told him she was pregnant. He had seemed like a nice enough guy she thought, a public defense lawyer in fact. They had been seeing each other just a couple months at the time. She had started to think that he might be 'the one'. He fit her checklist: good-looking, intelligent, good sense of humor, good job, etc. He was kind-hearted, laughed easily, and they had enjoyed what seemed like a relationship that was blossoming into something more than just dating. They hadn't discussed children, but he seemed so sweet Maria couldn't have imagined he'd react like he did. She admitted to being devastated when, after telling him, he suddenly stopped returning her calls.

Apparently, lawyer-client confidentiality extends to other lawyers as well, because when she called his office, the receptionist very curtly informed her that he, "...no longer works here. That's all I can tell you." His phone was 'no longer in service', and his apartment belonged to someone else within a week. She had never met his parents or family and, in fact, had no idea how to find them. He had said he was from New York City. Rather than perhaps hopelessly pursuing a man who obviously did not want to be a father, Maria decided she would have the child and raise her baby on her own.

"It was as much my decision as his to be sexually involved. Sometimes children are a consequence of sex. I couldn't very well chase him to the ends of the earth, trying to get him to take responsibility for something that was as much my fault as his. He made his decision about how to handle it and I made mine." She had planned to have children someday, so why not? Maria shifted the subject to Gooby and why he wasn't married.

This was always a subject Gooby had been very guarded about with the guys, but he felt comfortable with Maria—something that didn't happen too often for him around women he found attractive.

Gooby was uncomfortable with self-disclosure but he mentally gritted his teeth and told Maria about him and his high school sweetheart, Kim, with whom he had a long relationship through and after college. She had been his first real girlfriend and he, her first boyfriend. They had gone to the same college, he for computer science and she for business. When they had gotten their first real jobs, they bought a house together. They weren't married yet, but that seemed just an inevitable detail by then. The hold-up had always been Kim's. Goob had been all for getting married shortly after graduation, but Kim wanted to get her career started. Being the assistant manager of a chain restaurant that allowed patrons to throw peanut shells on the floor was not Kim's idea of big success in the business world. Goob had gotten his first job out of college at St. Bernard's General Hospital in their Information Technology department.

When St. Bernard's closed five years ago, University Hospital, well aware of Gooby's brilliance in designing the electronic records system for St. Bernard's, quickly snapped him up to do the same for them. Eventually, inevitably, they got married. It was what they were destined to do as far as anyone else could tell. But, as always happens, shortly after the wedding came the questions from friends and family.

"When are you two going to have a baby?"

"You waited so long to get married—shouldn't you be getting pregnant already?"

The problem was that it wasn't Gooby that would be getting pregnant—it was Kim. While Gooby was settling into his job running the I.T. department, Kim was busy climbing the corporate ladder. Seminars and trips to visit other corporations to study their business models kept her working long hours or gone on business trips more often that Goob would have liked. It also put off the baby conversation a little longer. Kim always had one more goal, one more 'project' she had to complete at work. The baby could wait six more months, she always said. Gooby began to feel frustrated and more distant from Kim. He seemed to be taking a back seat in her life to her career and their life together didn't seem so certain anymore.

As Kim's late hours and business trips became more the norm than the exception, Gooby developed his own life and interests outside of work, joining a golf league, going out with friends, and worrying less and less what Kim was doing. He was head of the I.T. department and was well compensated for his work. He was comfortable. At home however, he wasn't comfortable. He was lonely. Even when Kim was home and they were together, their togetherness didn't seem the way it had in the past. The time apart and almost separate lives they were leading took its toll on their relationship and sex life as well. When they did become intimate, there seemed to be very little intimacy in it. Their sex was infrequent and almost seemed something they did because they were supposed to. The cuddling and soft talk afterwards seemed forced and awkward. It was during these times that Gooby inevitably brought up the baby discussion. He fervently wanted to be a father and was worried that her career would never allow it. It was during one of these talks after sex that Kim angrily burst out, "Don't you get it? I love my job. I love my career. It's you I don't love! If I did, don't you think I'd be home more? Don't you think we'd have a baby by now? It's not what I want!"

Although she later apologized for how she said it, Kim couldn't take it all back. She said she loved Gooby, but that she didn't want the white picket fence and soccer mom life that Gooby was envisioning for her. It was after this discussion that they had their first real conversation in about three years. Unfortunately, that talk helped them realize that they wanted to go in different directions at this point in their lives. They had parted amicably, but Gooby was heartbroken at the thought that he was starting over at thirty-four, and might never have the chance to play a game of catch with his own son.

Unconsciously, Goob's eyes welled up as he told the story of his failed marriage. He was suddenly surprised by the touch of Maria's hand as she reached across the island to touch his. "Well it's a shame we didn't meet each other first," she said with a smile. "I'm about due for another margarita. How are you doing on your beer?"

They passed the next two hours sitting at the island in the kitchen, their empty plates still in front of them, talking, laughing, and suddenly feeling very fortunate to be neighbors. Their reverie was suddenly interrupted by music from Gooby's hip, *My blood runs cold, my memory has just been sold. My angel is the centerfold, angel is the centerfold.*

Gooby's face began to blush as he quickly answered his phone. "What? Holy shit! Ok, meet me at my dad's house... Oh, ok, I'll be right there. I'm just down the street at Maria's." Goob turned to Maria. "I'm sorry but I've got to go. I swear to God that if they weren't my friends, I'd kill them. They've got some big computer problem I have to help with. It's kind of urgent." In his nervousness, Gooby was talking a little too rapidly. "Thanks for the lunch and the conversation. It was nice."

Maria walked him to the door. "It's too bad I'm taking Josh to the movies tonight. I'd love to see you again. Maybe tomorrow?"

"Umm, yeah, I'd like that," he managed to stammer. He felt as if his tongue was suddenly twice its size in his mouth. He always felt like this around women. *Damn*, he thought to himself. *I hope she doesn't notice what a moron I sound like.* As he reached for the doorknob, he felt her hand on his elbow.

"Dave, thanks for fixing my grill. I hope we can do this again."

He felt the warm curve of her breast against his arm as she leaned forward and planted a kiss on the corner of his mouth. Instantly aroused by the sensation, he paused for a moment, looking into Maria's brown eyes. Suddenly, he did something that surprised even him—he turned towards Maria and kissed her on the mouth, lingering a little longer than just a polite 'thank you' kiss, and putting his hand on the small of her back to hold her a little closer. She didn't pull away and her lips parted slightly as they met his. As they separated, their eyes met and Goob suddenly remembered why he was standing in Maria's doorway kissing her.

He stammered, "I'm sorry I've got to go. The guys are waiting for me."

Maria smiled. "I'm sorry you have to go too." This statement had the force of a punch to the diaphragm, knocking the wind out of Dave as he turned, stumbling a little on his way down Maria's front steps.

16
Cooper

As I looked down the hole where the ladder descended, I briefly considered whether or not I could get down and open the shed door to escape quickly enough without getting burned badly. Unfortunately the flames, like flickering orange snakes, crept across the floor to the bottom of the ladder as I considered this course of action. Heat and thick, oily black smoke began to fill the lower floor of the shed and wafted upwards, forcing Cliff and me away from the opening. "Shit," Cliff said. "We're totally fucked. We have to find a way out of here."

We were trapped. Our only path of escape was already blocked by fire. It was getting dangerously hot and difficult to breath. I could see the evil little snakes of fire crawling up the ladder, their orange tongues seeking nourishment, fuel for the fire. This old, dry shed was burning fast. Cliff started to cough from the smoke that was quickly filling the loft. My eyes were starting to burn and water. We were going to have to make our own way out. I paused, considering what tools of escape we might have up here.

There wasn't much up here but the camping equipment. That was it! There had to be a camp shovel or hatchet up here. If the wood this shed was made of was dry enough to burn this fast, it was also dry enough to break through if we had the right tools. "Cliff," I half coughed, half yelled out. "Help me feel around. Look for an ax or shovel." It was a race against time. The flickering orange tongues of fire were licking at the lip of the opening to the loft. We had maybe a minute before they began to crawl across the floor, taking away our room to move and what little breathable oxygen was left. Cliff and I both began rummaging through everything, throwing the useless refuse in the direction of the fire, hoping to slow it, to put extra fuel in its way to consume before we were the only fuel left.

Sweat poured off me as I tried to rub the smoke from my eyes. My spirit soared as I heard a click of metal against metal when I threw a tarp aside. As quickly as my hope mounted, it crashed as I uncovered only pots and pans. Cliff seemed to be becoming disoriented. He was closer to the fire than I was and he seemed to be throwing things from his side into mine. On his hands and knees he was staggering, ready to collapse. Suddenly, my hand closed around a long, smooth, round handle. I grasped it as tightly as I could and pulled it free from the collapsed remains of the old Coleman stove. A shovel. It was the old, telescoping-handle shovel we used to dig trenches around our tents to prevent the rainwater from seeping underneath and soaking our sleeping bags as we slept. It would have to do.

Cliff was almost uselessly flailing around behind me. I pulled him towards me, and pulled both of us to the far end of the loft. "Stay close to me," I shouted. I couldn't tell if Cliff understood as he barely nodded. I then broke into a coughing fit as the burning, acrid smoke filled my lungs. I expelled my breath and sucked in one last, shallow gasp of air and smoke before I turned and drove the head of the small shovel into the wall. Nothing. It barely chipped a sliver out of it. I didn't dare inhale again. I again pulled the shovel back with both arms and drove it into the wall. As the pointed head of the shovel hit the wall, I thought I heard a crack, but I also heard something else. The small, round, metal cap that covered the end of the handle popped off and clattered to the floor. With it fell a flash drive—a three-inch-long, gray, computer flash drive. For some reason, as it briefly tumbled through the air from inside the shovel handle to the floor, my mind registered that it had Memorex printed on the side. It was barely visible through the smoke. It almost slipped out of my reach as I grasped for it and then shoved it into my pocket.

Cliff looked barely able to keep his eyes open as he slumped against the wall and weakly gestured with his hand in the direction of the flames, which were hastily encroaching upon what space remained for us. My lungs burned painfully as they screamed to my brain for more oxygen. There was no more oxygen to be found up here. I turned again with the shovel and drove it with all my strength and the weight of my body behind it into the wall again. This time I broke through. A small crack of daylight shone through where I had penetrated. I quickly moved forward and sat on my ass in front of the sliver of light. I leaned back and braced myself with my hands and then drove both feet forward at the crack I had made. I kicked hard enough to cause pain in my heels, but not hard enough to do more than break away a small piece of the wall. A crack, maybe ten inches tall and two inches wide, was not enough.

I felt myself getting dizzy. I wanted to rest, to lie down and sleep. Suddenly, an intense bolt of heat and pain shot through me as a tendril of flame caught my leg in its fiery grasp for a moment. The cool, fresh air that was rushing in through the crack I had made was feeding the fire, speeding its march across the last few feet of the loft. I pulled back, shocked to my senses. There was only about four feet of the loft that remained. Four feet that had not yet been devoured by the fire. I started to drag Cliff with me against the wall. I grabbed him around the chest like a lifeguard pulling a half-drowned swimmer from the pool. With Cliff in my grasp, I gave one last heave with my shoulder against the crack. Nothing. It didn't move. I slumped against the wall in despair. As I did so, the last of the oxygen I held in my lungs was spent. I exhaled and involuntarily sucked in a mouthful of scorching heat and gritty smoke. Almost overwhelmed by the pain in my lungs, I barely heard the wall slowly split and give way as Cliff and I tumbled out of the loft and landed with a painful thud in a heap on the ground eight feet below.

The sudden rush of seemingly cold air filling our lungs revived us. I was at first confused and disoriented— not sure what had happened. Quickly my mind began to clear and we rolled and crawled further away from the shed, which was now completely engulfed in flames. I reached down and felt my pocket. The flash drive was still there. I could still hear the crackling of flames and sirens in the distance as I passed out while lying exhausted on the lawn.

17

Cliff and I let ourselves into Goob's dad's house when we got there. Cliff gave Goob a quick call. "Hey Goob, sorry to interrupt your booty call, but someone tried to kill us again. Get your ass back to your dad's house. We found something."

Goob arrived a few minutes later. As he entered, I stood up holding the flash drive between my thumb and forefinger with a big, shit-eating grin on my face. "Holy shit, where'd you get that?" he exclaimed.

"Goob, it's not your dad's flash drive," I said.

Cliff and I told the story of our afternoon, concluding with, "So while you were off getting your dick wet, we were risking our lives *again,* trying to find out who's killing our parents."

Goob laughed. "Hey, don't blame me. It was Cooper's idea that I go on this mission. How do you know Maria wasn't going to try to kill me?"

We laughed as Cliff reached over to rub a tiny red smear on the corner of Goob's mouth. "Well, unless she was trying to kill you with lipstick, I think Coop and I had a little bit tougher time of it this afternoon than you did."

"Our dad's must have all had a flash drive. You guys ready to crack this open and see what we're up against?" I asked. I handed Goob the flash drive as he walked over to the computer.

No matter what the circumstances, he was always Gooby. "Hey, I hope you guys didn't sit on the good furniture in those filthy, smoky clothes," he said.

Unfortunately for Goob, he had grown up in one of those homes with a 'show living room'. You know, one of those living rooms that were strictly for entertaining guests and off limits for the kids. His parents kept the furniture covered in plastic and had plastic floor runners to protect the carpet when the room wasn't in use. Goob wasn't as compulsive about neatness as his mom, but he had inherited some of her tendencies. This tendency was a mixed blessing for Gooby. Yes, he did have an immaculately clean house, which women loved about him, but the downside was that he had to put up with a fair amount of ribbing from us about what this tendency might say about him. He wouldn't admit it, but I think Gooby is the type of guy who wishes he had a tiny closet so he could hang up all his socks on the hangers they came on from the store.

Cliff and I made eye contact behind his back and smirked because of course we had sat on the good furniture. We all reveled in being life-long best friends, but we also reveled in being the bane of each other's existence.

Goob plugged the flash drive into the small, ready-made port on the front of the computer. As with the other flash drive, the box appeared onscreen with FLASHDRIVE (J): Denial. We were not surprised by the title this time, but there was one difference that floored us, and made us ecstatic at the same time. There was no request for a password to access the information on the drive. "Hmm…, that's strange," Gooby said, "There's no password. No encryption. Nothing. We can just open it up."

With a bit of a chuckle I said, "Well, your dad hid the info his way and my dad hid it his way. You know my dad. He was just old school. He probably figured that no one would ever find it inside a shovel handle in the top of the shed. He was right, wasn't he?"

As we all waited holding our breath, Gooby clicked on the word Denial. It had haunted me since the moment I had found that eerie writing on my notepad. My dad had wanted me to know, and now here it was. The file opened and appeared to be an old document that had been scanned into a computer memory and then transferred to this flash drive. The yellowing of the paper from the scanned copy was still visible. I told you my dad was old school; he was probably still using that scanner until this week.

1
The Apocalypse Tribes

"The Apocalypse Tribes, as they are known, are believed to have been formed as part of an atheist movement in Europe during the 19th century. With the Scientific Movement beginning to make inroads with the general population, more and more citizens began to believe that the discoveries of evolutionary science directly contradicted most organized religions belief in a benevolent deity. While many people felt that Charles Darwin's hypothesis that man evolved from primates essentially erased the line between man and beast, The Apocalypse Tribes seemed to revel in and celebrate this belief. Although atheists are typically content to voice their assertion that there is no higher power, being, or deity, The Apocalypse Tribes have been accused of acts of terrorism against organized religion, especially The Church of England, several times throughout history.

The Apocalypse Tribes differ from typical atheist sects in that they believe it is for the good of mankind that their beliefs must overcome the ancient organized religions. History has seen its share of religious zealotry. The Apocalypse Tribes are zealots against religion, purporting that the belief in a deity responsible for the creation and direction of mankind is dangerous. The Apocalypse Tribes were founded on the premise that to delude ourselves into believing that there is salvation or life after death is to give up our responsibility for this, our only life. They have waged war against organized religion for centuries and have tried to intellectualize their cause by using former Russian Dictator Karl Marx's' famous quote, "religion is the opiate of the masses," as their war cry.

During the early 20th century, The Apocalypse Tribes seemed to fade into obscurity as the Industrial Revolution appeared to be sweeping away mankind's resistance to a lifestyle that was governed by the laws of science and progress.

Wartime, however, also fosters a return to religion as parents and wives pray for peace and the return of young men abroad. During the second half of the 20th century, America was seemingly perpetually at war, World War II, in Korea, Vietnam, and with the Soviet Union, before moving into the never-ending conflicts of the Middle East. The return of religious faith brought on by these wars was followed by the return of The Apocalypse Tribes, led by a vocal, charismatic survivalist named Jeffrey Warren.

Jeffrey Warren was an American who preached that people must prepare themselves for the inevitable World War III. He and his followers believed that only those prepared for the nuclear war would survive it. They did not believe praying to a God would stop these events from happening, nor did they believe that only those pious enough in life would be spared by their chosen deity at the last moment. It was by fueling these fears of nuclear war that Jeffrey Warren developed a faithful following in the 1970s and 1980s before apparently disappearing from public life under the threat of arrest.

The reason for the authorities' pursuit of Jeffrey Warren is well documented. He and his followers not only advocated a 'survival of the fittest' philosophy, but they applied these principals to their small, private communities as well. It was their beliefs regarding the treatment of children that drew the attention of Child Protective Services and the F.B.I. The Apocalypse Tribes often ran afoul of the law by violating child labor laws. Their beliefs in this regard are rather archaic. The Apocalypse Tribes are usually groups of families, sometimes small in numbers, but also sometimes quite large, which settle in mostly secluded rural towns. Much like Amish communities, the Tribes keep to themselves and try to be as self-sufficient as possible by farming and making or building as many of their own supplies as possible. Children are often used as unpaid laborers as soon as they are old enough to manage the tasks that are required of them. The children never attend public schools and The Tribes have always maintained that they homeschool their children to prevent them from falling prey to the negative public perception of The Tribes.

During the 1980s, as public attention and legal scrutiny of The Apocalypse Tribes peaked, the allegations of sexual abuse against the children of The Tribes also arose. Jeffrey Warren vehemently denied these charges, claiming that the federal authorities had fed this false information to the media in an effort to discredit his movement. With Child

Protective Services attempting to investigate The Tribes,
whenever they could find a group, and the F.B.I. pursuing
tax-evasion charges against The Tribes as a whole and
Jeffrey Warren individually, the fiery leader stopped
making public appearances in 1986. By 1990, The
Apocalypse Tribes had seemingly disappeared and were
largely forgotten. Authorities never located Jeffrey Warren
after his last public appearance."

"Hmmmm... now this is interesting," Gooby said.
"Look at this." Following the scanned news report were
two lists. The first was a list of names of families that had,
or still did, live in our neighborhood. The list had no title or
any type of notation indicating what its' purpose was. Were
these members of an *Apocalypse Tribe*, or were they
enemies? The second list was much more cryptic. The
second list contained the names of members of our
neighborhood who had died and the month and year of their
deaths. There were a dozen names with dates going back to
the early 1970s. Some of the names were on both lists, but
some were not. The most recent entry was Gooby's dad a
week ago. If this shocked or upset him, Gooby didn't show
it.

I suddenly had to have possession of the flash drive.
Until his death, my father had kept this record of what was
apparently a hidden war between our parents and an
Apocalypse Tribe. But why? What had our parents died
fighting against? Why didn't they just report *The Tribe* to
the authorities? There was something more to this that we
were missing. If my father had thought this important
enough to keep, then I would to keep it as well. As if that
weren't nearly enough, I nearly died trying to find this. I
wasn't about to lose this flash drive, or this war.

SLAM! We all nearly jumped out of our skin, fists up, ready to defend ourselves against another attack. "Hey guys! Where are you?" Chuck shouted. He had gotten off duty and headed straight over to see what we were up to.

"We're in here, Chuck," I shouted. "Grab a cold beer and a chair. You're going to want to sit down for this."

Always consistent, Chuck did grab a beer and walked in, setting his chair down backwards so he could rest his arms on the back as he straddled it. Before we could start to tell Chuck about what we found, Cliff, whose ability to heap ridicule on anyone at any time never fails, started in on him. "Jeez, thanks Chuck. Get yourself a beer and ignore the rest of us, why don'tcha? Didn't your parents teach you any manners?"

Chuck gave his familiar helpless grimace and shook his head with a sigh. It was a look we had grown used to over the years since we were usually the cause of it. Cliff realized his mistake in mentioning Chuck's parents. "Sorry Chuck, don't worry about it. I'll get'em," Cliff said as he gave Chuck a pat on the shoulder and headed into the kitchen.

"You're lucky. If I wasn't so used to you being an ass, I might shoot you," Chuck shouted after him. Chuck seemed to be enjoying his newfound stature among our little group. It didn't matter, he was still Chuck to us, but if it made him happy to brag a little about his spy gig, then we'd let him have it now and then. We owed him. We were horrible to him as kids.

"Damn! You guys look like shit," Chuck said with a smirk. "And have you started smoking?"

Cliff just shook his head and said, "Shut up, dickhead. Do you want to hear about what happened or not?" As always that elicited a chuckle from Goob and me. Cliff and Chuck were always bickering, but they'd kill for each other in an instant. We all would really.

After we concluded our usual introductory stupidity, we all told Chuck about the events of the day. Gooby seemed to take particular delight in telling Chuck about his visit with Maria, and Chuck seemed to be equally annoyed hearing it. After we told our stories, we sat in silence as Chuck read what was on the flash drive. "Well, what do you think? " I said.

"So we've got ourselves an evil cult," Chuck replied. "This still isn't enough to convince anyone of anything. We're going to have to do this alone. I've got a few ideas that may help us turn the tables," he said with a smile. "I think it's time to kick some cult ass."

18

Night had begun to fall as we prepared ourselves for what might be a very eventful evening. All of us were dressed in black shirts with dark pants and sneakers. "Hey Chuck," I said. "I like you in black. Very slimming."

It was hard not to laugh at ourselves because this is what we used to do as kids when we went outside on warm summer nights to play 'commando'. We would lurk in the bushes around the neighborhood, peering in our neighbors' windows. Nothing perverted, mind you. We didn't have any neighbors we were interested in looking at in 'that way'. More often than not, all we observed were families sitting around their living rooms watching television. We imagined we were on the side of good, protecting the neighborhood from the evil that we believed must come out after dark in every neighborhood. Still, it felt very titillating to watch others when they didn't know they were being watched. Sometimes it was just the thrill of being out after dark, walking through our quiet, still neighborhood that seemed like another world when the light of day was long gone. More often than not, we went on these expeditions during the summer when we were sleeping out in one of our forts or a tent set up in someone's backyard.

As often as we had played our little spy games as kids, we were never lucky enough to stop, or even observe, any real criminal activity. We cursed our bad luck at living in such a wholesome All-American neighborhood. Little did we know at the time that we apparently were just really bad at sniffing out the bad guys. *Let's hope we're better at it now*, I thought as we headed out the door together.

The quick call to Christine had gone about as I expected it would. I had probably made a hundred of these calls over the years. "I'll be home later honey. Don't worry; I'll be with the guys." By now she knew better than to waste energy voicing resistance. Also, I think she knew that at a time like this, with our parents recently deceased, time with each other was exactly what the guys and I needed.

"Being with the guys is exactly what worries me. That never leads to anything good. Are you sure you're ok?" With my assurance that we were taking care of each other, I told her good night. I was lucky. Christine was the best. Why she puts up with me, I'll never know. I'm sure she wonders the same thing most days.

19

We all piled into Chuck's tiny, black Ford Mustang. It was definitely not a car meant to carry four grown men. Fortunately, we were very comfortable with each other. Since he joined the military, Chuck had chosen to live on base and spent his extra cash on fast cars. A few times, his love of classic muscle cars and speed had nearly cost him his life and just as importantly his placement in the Homeland Security Task Force. With its black exterior and with windows that were obviously tinted much darker than was legal, this car looked like it was meant to prowl the streets at night. Chuck was happy to tell us that his Mustang, after a few modifications of his own, could go 0-60 in about 5.2 seconds, making it one of the fastest cars on the road. It was at that moment that I, quickly joined by Cliff and Goob, briefly broke into the chorus of *Secret Agent Man*, which was originally done by The Ventures and more recently re-made by Blues Traveler.

Chuck and I had orchestrated the night's plan. We only had to go halfway around the block to drop off Cliff and Goob, who quickly slipped into the familiar shadows of our neighborhood and crept back into the bushes at the back of Gooby's dad's old yard. If everything went as expected, Cliff and Goob would have company before long.

I would have to be dropped off next before Chuck doubled back to park his car not too far from where he had dropped off the other guys. Our neighborhood was laid out like a small letter 'h'. Chuck killed the headlights, let off the gas, pushed in the clutch, and coasted quietly to a stop in the shadowy dead end that was the top part of the 'h'.

The end of the street was sheltered from the moonlight by towering oak trees that seemed to stretch across the street to hold their green, leafy hands in an arch above me. The moon was full and swollen with its luminescent glow casting shadows as if it were noon. I carefully opened the door and stepped out into the night. A warm breeze blew through the tops of the trees. In my black attire, I'm sure I was hardly visible. The cold parcel I was carrying was tucked securely under my arm.

Chuck eased up on the clutch ever so carefully and allowed the car to slowly roll back out of the dead end. As he pulled away, I turned to peer into the darkness ahead of me. The part in the trees ahead indicated that the trail was still there. What I was about to do violated every ethical standard I had ever promised to uphold. Then again, those bastards had killed my dad. All bets were off as far as I was concerned. Screw the ethics. They were not going to fuck with my family anymore.

I approached the trail as quickly and quietly as I possibly could; hoping to blend into the shadows before I was seen. The night had that magical quality it always seemed to have when we were kids. The only sounds were those of the leaves restlessly whispering in the treetops and the crickets calling out to each other. The night would have been perfect for a relaxing stroll with my dog. As I pushed a branch aside and began to creep noiselessly up the slightly muddy incline between the trees, I heard the sound I had been hoping for, laughter.

I immediately stepped sideways into the brush and crouched down before continuing my slow advance. As I neared the edge of the brush and peered between the branches, I began to see patches of the schoolyard illuminated as bright as day by the moonlight. Not ideal for later, but it would help me now. I cautiously leaned forward, fearful that my face could be seen between the leaves. Peering through the leaves made it seem as if I were looking through a telescope. In brief flashes I could see them as they ran, chasing each other up and over the slides and through the tunnels that were built for bodies much smaller than theirs. There were three of them, two teenage boys and a girl.

Some things never change. As adolescents, the guys and I had hung out on this very playground on many warm, summer nights. Only then the equipment was hard steel with no bed of woodchips to cushion our fall. The elementary school of my youth had joined the 21st century with a giant, brightly colored, plastic Habitrail of a playground that looked more appropriate for giant hamsters than children. When we were younger, we would go here at night to sit on the swings and talk in a place that seemed our own, and later, as older teens, we would steal away to this place with a few beers in each of our pockets. When we were even older, a couple of us even claimed our first sexual experiences here on top of the slide or underneath the monkey bars. Whether we intended it or not, losing our virginity on the playground was perhaps the purest, most symbolic way we could have marked our passage from childhood to adulthood. *These new, giant plastic monstrosities would certainly add a bit of creativity to that experience*, I thought to myself.

One boy tackled the girl and they all collapsed on the ground laughing. When they sat up, one of the boys lit a cigarette in his mouth and handed it to the girl. The girl appeared to be one of the 'goth' kids I had seen walking the neighborhood a few nights ago just before someone tried to run us down. Although their appearance is off-putting for most adults, through my experience as a therapist I had learned that most 'goth' kids are actually pretty nice kids who aren't spending their spare time making human sacrifices to Satan. Heck, half the time their parents had dragged them to therapy just because of their appearance.

Here I sat in the bushes, observing another group of teenage friends demonstrating their independence, or maybe rebelliousness, by frolicking on the playground after dark. I had to play this exactly right or I'd probably end up getting arrested, discredited professionally, and most likely divorced. I set the bag I was carrying down next to the base of the nearest tree and made a mental note of its distance from the trail. I pulled my hood up over my head, stood up, and stepped out into the glow of the moonlight. The laughter stopped as if it was a recording and someone had abruptly pushed the 'pause' button.

I tried to appear as relaxed as possible, as if I were merely out for a moonlit walk. The teens were milling about, suddenly subdued as they leaned in closely to whisper to each other. Self-consciously, I looked about as if I were missing a signal the teens had picked up on. I, an unknown adult, had intruded on their domain. I continued towards them. I hadn't thought out the details of this very far. I assumed it would be easy. Me, the great and powerful child therapist, would immediately be able to form a trusting bond, leading to the rebellious teens completely spilling their rebellious guts to me about *The Apocalypse Tribe* that was hiding beneath the idyllic surface of our neighborhood. I was an arrogant idiot. What the hell was I thinking? And what gave me the brilliant idea that I could bribe them with a twelve-pack of beer? FUCK! I was screwed. Why had I shot my mouth off to the guys that I could get the local teens to spill the beans on their evil, cult-loving parents? No, I didn't rhyme that on purpose. It just happens sometimes when I'm nervous.

Hmmm… actually, that doesn't sound like a bad idea. I had been right about the fact that I'd find some teenagers out here at night. What teenager didn't have a little anger towards their parents? My theory was this: Take an angry teen or two, parents with a secret, throw in a little alcohol, and voila! Someone gives up the goods on their folks to a sympathetic stranger. I realize that by planning to get kids drunk and manipulate them that I was almost as devious as the cult I was pursuing, but I wasn't going to murder anyone in cold blood.

These kids did seem old enough that they might like a beer. After all, they were already acting like they were high. If I was lucky, they might be. That would sure make this a lot easier. I just had to hope that some creepy old guy stepping out of the woods at night, offering them beer, wouldn't freak them out. *Ok, calm down. Stay cool*, I said to myself. I needed to convey just the right mix of calm, non-creepy confidence that wouldn't alarm them. What would I say? I was nearly to them and they seemed to be pacing about nervously. Their boisterous behavior gone as if they feared I was there to arrest them. If they thought I was a cop, there was no way they'd talk to me. I had to assume that if they were out here at night their parents didn't know it. I had to immediately reassure them that I wasn't a narc or a cop.

"Hey, have you guys seen my dog? It's a black lab named Robin. I was walking home from the mini-mart when the leash broke and she ran off," I said.

They looked at each other briefly before Pimple boy in the Metallica shirt said, "No, we haven't seen any dog. What does she look like?"

What does a black lab look like? Sheesh, these kids weren't rocket scientists. This might prove easier than I thought. "She's a medium-sized dog, all black. Probably hard to see at night, I know. Hey, do you kids hang out here very often?"

The goth girl spoke up this time. Like most goth teens, she had the long, straight, black hair with eyeliner and fingernails to match. Most of her clothes were black too. "What do you care? You're not a cop, are you?"

I laughed a little at this. "No, I'm not a cop. Come here, look at this."

I lead them over to the edge of the playground where the path entered between two old four inch by four inch wooden posts that had once held a gate. I pointed to the side of one of the posts about a foot above the ground. It has been painted over, but it was still there. Among the voluminous carvings on the old, wooden post was 'CS 88'.

I grinned and said, "Would a cop vandalize school property like that?" I had carved my initials and the year here on a night very much like this all those years ago. "You kids aren't the first to hang out here at night," I said.

Pimple boy looked incredulous. 'No way! That is not you! That is awesome. We have to do that!" Bingo! I had it. Trust. It was that easy. Now to reel in the big fish.

"I'm a little old to go back to a life of crime, but if you kids help me look around here for my dog, I'll split my twelve-pack with you. I left it over here. I set it down when I started to chase my dog." I trotted over to the edge of the trees and fetched the twelve-pack in the brown paper bag. As I walked back carrying the beer, the three kids looked back and forth at each other a little warily, but they also looked a little excitedly at the beer under my arm too. This was the moment of truth.

20
Chuck

Chuck coasted to a stop quietly about halfway between streetlights. He was in his element, and now he had his friends with him. As kids, they had spent countless summer nights on imaginary stakeouts in their neighborhood. Now it was for real. What could be more perfect? *I'm not going to blow it this time*, he thought. As he took a deep breath before he reached for the door, he realized that by sheer coincidence, or perhaps sheer karma, he had parked in front of the Kirstner's house.

He remembered when they had picked a night just like this all those years ago. The four of them were sleeping out in their fort. It wasn't really much of a fort, but it was a shelter of sorts that we had built by scavenging leftover wood and two by fours from a nearby construction site. Our field and woods would soon give way to more suburban sprawl, but we were ignorant of that fact despite the quickly multiplying new homes that were beginning to encroach upon our childhood world. Although our little fort was only located in the small copse of trees behind Gooby's property, we felt like we were on our own. It was like having our own apartment as kids. It was where we'd hide out and hang out, solving the mysteries of growing up. We probably would have called it quits early that night when the mosquitoes got to us, but unfortunately, we never got the chance to find out.

Like most kids growing up, we had worshipped the typical TV role models, superheroes, spies, cops with cool, and the like. As early adolescents however, we turned to mischief when left unsupervised. This was one of those nights.

The plan was almost perfect. It was the old ding and ditch, but with a twist. The smoke bomb would be carefully placed on the Kirstner's doorstep, lit, and then the bell would be rung. We would watch with malicious glee from our safe hiding places as they opened their door to a face full of smoke. Chuck was the youngest, and as part of his endless drive to gain our acceptance, to be regarded as an equal by the three older of us, he had volunteered for the task of lighting the smoke bomb and ringing the bell. He was supposed to do this carefully and quietly. What he did was not quiet or careful.

As he sat in his Mustang recalling that night, Chuck still cringed at the memory of tripping on the edge of the front stoop and banging his shoulder into the storm door, eliciting a loud noise that had drawn the attention of old man Kirstner. Determined not to let his friends down, he had quickly set down the smoke bomb and attempted to light it as old man Kirstner opened the door. He had been recognized as he attempted to run away. Old man Kirstner threatened to let his dog out. His dog was a large German Shepard with a neighborhood reputation for biting any kid who got too close while daring to tease or taunt it as it lay tied up in the yard. As Chuck froze at the thought of becoming a chew toy, old man Kirstner grabbed his arm. Chuck panicked and ratted us all out.

We had forgiven Chuck for that, but he had never forgotten, and he had never felt like he had won our unconditional acceptance as an equal member of *The*

Golden Boys. Chuck realized that he was a grown man and it was stupid to still be hoping to impress his peers, but as he sat in his sleek, black, phallic symbol, he gritted his teeth and vowed to return successfully.

Chuck shook himself from his reverie, took a deep breath, and carefully opened the car door, closing it with firm pressure rather than a push. He surveyed the street. At this time, the neighborhood appeared deserted. Windows were lit here and there as a few night owls stayed up, perhaps watching the new episode of CSI: Something or Other. Chuck had never really gotten into those nighttime soaps, but now he felt like he was living one.

He casually walked around the front of his car and onto the sidewalk, as if he were about to head to a front door to pick up his friend for a night on the town. Despite having carefully chosen his parking spot in the darkest area between streetlights, Chuck cast a shadow by the moonlight. He walked a short distance up the sidewalk before casually turning right off the sidewalk and behind the enormous pine tree growing at the front corner of Kirstner's yard. From here he could slip into the darkness and skirt the edge of the property until…Rowf! Rowr, rowr, rowr!

Chuck froze, his breath caught in his throat, his blood feeling as if it had stopped flowing in his veins. *No, it can't be,* he thought to himself. He stepped back into the Douglas fir and trained his eyes on the front of the house. There, by the corner of the house. The backyard was fenced, but at the corner barking as if his hindquarters were on fire, was a German Shepard.

"Schottzie! Shut up. What's wrong with you?" SLAM! The door shut again and the dog quieted momentarily. Chuck moved quickly, striding towards the fence and holding out his hand with a dog biscuit. Schottzie met him at the corner of the fence, his warm, wet nose pushed through the diamond-shaped links to sniff his new friend with the peace offering.

This was no ordinary dog biscuit. Dog biscuits were standard equipment for any covert operative in the Homeland Security Agency, but Chuck had taken special precautions. He had taken the time to soak his dog biscuits in root beer-flavored Schnapps, twice, giving them an extra-sedating quality. Obviously it was a wise move, but a little embarrassing that Chuck always had root beer Schnapps on hand.

Schottzie gobbled up three of the sweet, little offerings in one quick, greedy mouthful. "Sweet dreams pooch," Chuck whispered as he walked along the fence toward the back of the property. Schottzie happily followed his new best friend as far as the fence would allow before Chuck flipped him one last, tasty treat and stepped into the row of trees dividing this yard from the one behind it.

21

Cliff

Goob and Cliff casually ambled down the well-worn path between the houses as if they were out for a nightly stroll. The only clue that they might not be out to enjoy an evening constitutional was the fact that their clothing was matching black pants and shirts from head to toe. The path was on a twelve-foot-wide strip of land between the houses that was bordered by tall, unkempt hedges on both sides. It ran perpendicularly, connecting the two parallel streets. The land belonged to the town, allowing workers access to sewer and electric lines underground. Very few residents were aware of this fact, but over the years, going back to before we could remember, the neighborhood kids had figured out that they could cut through to the other street without any complaint, resulting in the now-aged path they walked. The kids never questioned or wondered why. It was just one of those things about their neighborhood that had always been so. The path was a permanent feature of the neighborhood and was so frequently used that it may not ever have had any grass growing upon it.

As adults, we often forget that every neighborhood has a hidden infrastructure of paths and places that only the kids know about. I still remember the path to *The Pond* and the trail that would take us to and through *The Woods*. All of the secret, hidden kid places had simple names that we all knew them by. It was part of the language that each neighborhood has. A language developed over generations of kids spending their days, and sometimes nights, playing in that hidden infrastructure. When we were younger, these were our secret places where we felt that we were the kings of our world. No adult had ever stepped foot in our world. During the long, dog days of summer, these secret places were witness to countless childhood dramas that our parents were never aware of. Sometimes we built forts hidden deep in the woods from where we could plan our covert operations against competing groups of like-minded kids, or we would just sit in the privacy of our home away from home, using our group wisdom to plumb the depths of the childhood challenges we all faced. We would tease, talk, and learn from each other as we grew up. Now the hidden infrastructure of our neighborhood would serve as our ally in a much more important war than those epic battles we waged as kids.

Gooby and Cliff had taken part in plenty of fake stakeouts when we were kids, but it was never our own homes we were staking out. Chuck's idea, which was to go into the room where we had left the 'live' bug and talk about going out tonight, was perfect. We'd get a chance to see who, if anyone, broke into the house to either take something or attempt to set up another death trap.

After cautiously skirting the back of the neighbor's yard and slipping into the shadows, Cliff and Goob settled into their hiding spot underneath the large, yellow-flowered forsythia bush in the back corner of Gooby's yard. *This is one friggin' huge bush*, Cliff thought to himself as they crouched and forced their way underneath.

The same branches that scratched at their faces and pulled at their clothing as they crawled under the bush would also be their best cover. "Thank God your dad wasn't Edward Scissorhands," Cliff said. Cliff and Goob lay on their stomachs under the bush, completely concealed from view by darkness and the overhanging branches.

"Man, this sucks," Gooby said. "Why are we stuck lying in the dirt under a bush while those two are out having fun? I'm going to smell like wet grass for a week. I'm going to have to shower up before we go to O'Brien's later."

Again, thanks to Chuck, Goob was spy equipped with a pair of night-vision binoculars. Unfortunately, Chuck only had one pair. "C'mon Goob," Cliff whined in a whisper, "let me look through them."

After an exaggerated, heavy sigh of exasperation, Gooby replied, "How about this—we'll both take fifteen minutes at a time. It's not like you can't see anything with your own two eyes. Shut up and pay attention."

"Ok, it's 9:32. I want my turn at 9:47," Cliff whispered as he gave Goob a little elbow in the ribs. He couldn't see it, but Gooby was seriously rolling his eyes behind the binoculars.

"So Goob," Cliff whispered, "do you really like Maria, or are you just being a pain in the ass to Chuck?" An exasperated, and possibly exaggerated sigh, issued from Cliff's immediate right. Goob didn't turn his head and appeared to be pretending that he didn't hear the question. "C'mon Goob, I know you can hear me. You can tell me. I won't say anything to Chuck or Cooper."

This last statement elicited another sigh and this time, Gooby turned his head to look Cliff right in the eyes through the darkness. "You mean you won't tell them just like you didn't tell them when I found out I was having cyber-sex with a dude?"

Cliff unsuccessfully attempted to stifle a giggle. "Oh c'mon, you know there was no way any of us would have kept that secret. I told you never to believe those pictures people put up on *MySpace*."

"You would have fallen for it too." Gooby said, "He was really good at sounding like he was a girl."

Cliff didn't even attempt to stifle his laughter this time and, much to Goob's chagrin, he had only been momentarily distracted before returning to his original line of questioning. "Yeah, yeah, yeah. So what's the deal with you and Maria? Are you really interested in her?"

Before Gooby could roll his eyes, he felt a sharp, small stab in one of his thighs that caused him to drop the binoculars.

At almost the same moment Cliff exclaimed, "What the *fuck*?"

As Gooby began to roll over to look behind him, the world suddenly appeared as if it were underwater. The smell of dirt and damp grass filled his nose as his head became too heavy to keep up. The last thing he saw before blacking out was Cliff, apparently out cold, on the ground beside him.

The two men stood behind the large bush, concealed by trees and the shadows of the night. As they looked down at the pair of feet sticking out from beneath the bush, the darkly clad figure on the left said, "What do we do with'em now?"

Darkly clad figure number two replied, "We gotta bring'em back. It's not up to us. You got the rope?"

"Yeah, I got it," number one answered. "How long does this stuff last?"

The two darkly clad figures carried their load with the casual confidence of men who were behaving as if they had every right in the world to be where they were, doing what they were doing. On this quiet, sleepy suburban street most residents were likely settled in for the evening, debating who should be *the next American Idol!* As with most lifetime suburbanites, everyone had already tucked themselves safely into their white-picket prisons, falsely assuming that because they could turn a deadbolt; their world was safe for another day. The men had little fear of being noticed, much less questioned. Then again, this was a neighborhood in which few would choose to question them anyway.

Had Gooby been conscious, their arrogance would have completely pissed him off. When they reached the car they rather unceremoniously dumped their burden into the trunk. "Hey," darkly clad figure number two said, "you think we got enough time for a beer at O'Brien's before we head back?" The unremarkable, four-door sedan quietly pulled away from the curb and almost casually trundled down the street in the direction of O'Brien's.

22

Cooper

The three teens eyed me warily, but their eyes also got as big as saucers and they snuck furtive glances at each other as I took the beer out of the bag and set it on the ground. I pulled out a bottle, twisted the cap off, and casually took a swig. "Go ahead. Help yourselves."

Goth Girl and Pimple Face looked at each other, trying hard to suppress their apparent glee. Before reaching for a beer, they looked to the third boy. *He must be the unofficial leader of this little group*, I thought. He was the one I would have to sweet talk. Nothing would get said by the other two without his approval. He was average looking, with a slightly shaggy, skater-type hairstyle. He was dressed in ragged jeans with a concert t-shirt and a long-sleeve thermal undershirt. He walked with the gait of an athlete and carried himself with a quiet, unpretentious confidence that was unusual in teens. He paused and then nodded to the other two as he reached into the box for a beer.

I was in. This was the moment. Taking the beer was a sign of trust. "Why don't we leave the twelve here while we look for my dog?" We paired up, with Pimple Face and me searching the border of one half of the playground and Goth Girl and Leader Boy going the other direction. I figured that Goth Girl would gravitate toward Leader Boy and that Leader Boy would likely be the strongest personality of the three.

I intentionally angled to get myself paired up with Pimple Face, whose name turned out to be Josh. I figured that with his slight build and his acne he probably wasn't the high school definition of confidence, and thus might prove easier to persuade into talking if he felt he was getting some type of approval. As we ambled along the edge of the playground, we beat the bushes and shouted out the name of a dog we would never find. I watched Josh finish his beer and took a brief detour to grab us each another one. As we walked, I learned his name and that he had lived in the neighborhood since he was two. He was in the 10th grade.

I talked about my experiences in the neighborhood as a teenager and the things my friends and I used to do right here on this very playground. To garner a little more trust and provide an opening for Josh, I talked about my parents, falsifying stories of their frequent odd hours and errands that allowed me to go out at night with my friends. I felt bad about this, but I even implied some vague abuse in an effort to up the ante. Eventually Josh talked about himself. His folks were still alive and married, and seemed to have some of the same strange nocturnal habits my parents had. *BINGO! Now I'm getting somewhere*, I thought. Fortunately the light of the moon wasn't bright enough for Josh to see the look of eagerness as I hung on his every word. As Christine will tell you, I'm not much of an actor. And no, I'm not referring to our sex life.

I asked Josh what he thought his parents nighttime excursions might be about, and he immediately seemed guarded, even furtive. He stammered a little, "I-I can't really say. They don't like when I ask questions."

I had to push the envelope a little further. I had to get more. In the distance I could hear Josh's friends calling out my dog's name. I couldn't keep this charade up much longer before I ran out of beer and the kids lost interest. "So Josh," I said, "I take it your parents are members of *The Tribe* too?"

20

Chuck

Chuck peered at Maria's house from the cover of the hedgerow. With the exception of the front porch light, the house was dark. As Cooper had said, Maria appeared to be gone for the evening. Chuck cautiously skirted the hedges and then the wooden fence, moving stealthily until he reached the back patio. With the house apparently empty, he realized that he probably could have strolled up the front walk, but he had been taught to never underestimate the potential danger of any situation. Thus far *The Apocalypse Tribe* had proved to be far more dangerous than he would have expected.

That's what doesn't fit, he thought. These are supposed to be survivalist nut cases who hate organized religion. We're not the government pursuing them and none of our parents are particularly religious, so why are they trying to kill us? We're missing some piece of the puzzle. He doubted that Maria's house would yield any clues, but it couldn't hurt to take a look around now that the chance presented itself.

The single back door to the garage appeared to be his most likely avenue of entrance. The lock was not a deadbolt and he picked it easily enough. If some highly motivated and intelligent burglars wanted to make a killing, they should really spend more time in the suburbs. Then again, if the individuals were intelligent and highly motivated, they probably wouldn't be burglars.

Inside the garage, Chuck donned his infrared goggles and suddenly the night appeared well lit, albeit in shades of green. The garage appeared as normal as any other with the requisite lawnmower, bicycles, rakes, and shovels. There were but a few small shelves, covered with empty flowerpots and cans of spray paint, affixed to one wall. A quick walk around the garage revealed nothing suspicious. Chuck noted the electric garage-door opener hanging from the rafters. The noise of the garage door opening would provide him with a warning should Maria and Josh return while he was still in the house.

As Chuck expected, the door from the garage was unlocked and he walked into the kitchen. *This sucks*, he thought to himself. *There's no way one person can do a thorough search of a house in the amount of time I've got.* He knew there was no other way. *Hmmm...where are the most likely places to hide things?* He wasn't sure what he was looking for, but he didn't think it would be anything large. *First the computer, and then, Maria's a woman, so... back of the underwear drawer or top of the closet it's got to be.*

He found the computer easily in the family room by the front door, but a quick search of the desk and its contents revealed nothing but the usual day-to-day bills and printed-out pictures. Chuck knew he wouldn't have time to do a thorough search of the computers files, so he decided to move on. Getting caught breaking the law when it wasn't part of his job would definitely not go over well with his superiors.

After painfully clipping his shin on a coffee table and tripping over what he assumed was a pair of Josh's shoes, Chuck found his way to the stairs and up to Maria's room. He slipped the infrared goggles off and put them into his pocket. *I can probably look around safely enough with my penlight*, he thought. Chuck swept the tiny light around the room, surveying his surroundings. The bedroom looked definitely feminine, but ordinary enough. The queen-sized bed sat in the middle of the room. It was a four-post bed with a lacey canopy above it. It was unmade. The master bath was off to the left of the bed. The dresser was a low, long model that sat against the wall across from the foot of the bed. There were two windows, one on either side of the bed, but they were curtained and Chuck doubted that anyone would notice the flickering illumination of his tiny penlight. The closet was to the right in the corner.

Chuck walked over to the closet and carefully slid the double doors open. Thankfully, it wasn't a walk-in. A top shelf ran the width of the closet and was covered with a few shoes boxes and sweaters. It took about two minutes to ascertain that the shoeboxes contained nothing but shoes. Apparently Maria was fond of expensive stiletto heels. As he was putting a pair of black, three-inch heel, Bruno Magli's back in their exquisitely tailored box, Chuck caught himself imagining Maria's legs in a pair of sexy stockings with these heels on. The thought of stockings reminded Chuck that he intended to search the dresser as well. He completed his search of the top and bottom of the closet without finding anything more interesting, or relevant, than the sexy shoes.

The dresser had four drawers across the top row. Chuck decided to search left to right. It appeared that Maria was as logical as the next person and, much to Chucks' delight, had put her underwear in the first drawer on the left. Chuck held the penlight in his teeth so he could have both hands free for his search. As he eagerly thrust his hands into Maria's drawers, he got that familiar feeling again. The soft, smooth feel of lace, silk, and satin under his hands caused a stirring in his loins that he found hard to resist. Chuck tried to focus on the job at hand. He reminded himself he was here because someone had killed his father, and Cooper's and Goob's too. He was looking for clues as he had done so many other times. He had also done this many other times too.

He took a pair of panties out and held them up to the light in front of him. A pair of red, satin, string bikinis with a little bow on the low-slung front. He eyed them and his imagination began on a journey it had traveled before. *No!* Chuck shouted in his head. *I have to get what I came for and get out. Getting caught isn't worth this now*. He quickly shoved the panties in his pocket and continued his search. The first drawer contained nothing but the collection of sexy panties, the second bras, and the third stockings. No fishnet thigh highs as Chuck had imagined, *but sexy nonetheless*, he thought.

Cooper

Chuck was a total 'horndog', which is what we often called him. His radar was on 24/7 and it was amazing he had never given himself whiplash craning his neck to get a better look at a woman. He did rear end a parked car once though. I'd swear he had the neck of an owl. It seemed that if a woman walked by, he could turn his head 180 degrees to follow her with his eyes. If his eyes could have done that 'Aaaah Ooogah!' thing that cartoon characters do with their eyes, I wouldn't have been surprised in the least. As it was, if a pretty pair of eyes, legs, or anything else walked by, he immediately looked as if he had a thyroid condition. Needless to say, this over-eager behavior usually scared them off.

He was still single and quite possibly doomed to be forever. He was totally and completely into women. Unfortunately, his calm and cool under pressure in his job did not carry over when he found himself confronted with the opportunity to talk to a woman he found attractive. His brain became completely unglued and suddenly he morphed into Rainman, repeating "I'm an excellent driver" or whatever fumbling attempt at a pick-up line he came up with at the moment. He was a source of endless amusement for the rest of us when we went out together.

Chuck

The fourth top drawer contained belts. None of the drawers seemed to contain anything remotely related to any crazy cult killings. Chuck was about to leave the room when his eyes saw something. There it was on the corner of the dresser, among the decorative scented candles and the pictures of Maria and Josh. He couldn't believe it. All this time he had been searching as if the clues were hidden. He had made a rookie mistake. He was thinking that because Maria had something to hide that she would hide it. He forgot what he learned in his Criminal Psychology class. Criminals are usually arrogant. They always assume they will get away with things until they are caught. They assume that they are smarter than those who might pursue them.

"You know what they say when you assume?" Chuck hated when some moron blurted out that phrase in a meeting as he was speaking, but as he knew, more often than not it was true. Usually a criminal's arrogance makes them do stupid things, such as leave evidence of their crimes out in the open. Chuck picked up the flash drive, stuck it in his pocket, and headed for the stairs.

As his foot hit the first step he heard the sound he had feared. The garage door opening! They were coming in the way he had entered. *FUCK! I've got to find a way out!* Chuck thought. *Damn it. I don't know what to do. I'm usually the one doing the pursuing.* He could hear first one car door, then the other, slam shut. The door from the garage to the kitchen opened.

"Hey Mom, can I have a snack?"

"No Josh. You just had popcorn at the movies. It's late. You've got to get to bed."

Chuck quickly evaluated his options for a hiding spot. Both Maria and Josh's rooms were out of the question. That left the hall bathroom. But what if Josh came in? Chuck carefully edged the Spongebob shower curtain back as carefully as possible and stepped into the tub, silently moving to the other end to obscure himself from view.

"Don't forget to brush your teeth either, Josh, and do a good job this time." The rapid pounding of little feet ascending the stairs made Chuck catch his breath, fearful that his quick, shallow respirations would give him away. Even through the shower curtain the room suddenly seemed ablaze with light. The toilet seat lifted and Chuck could hear Josh peeing. Slam! He put the seat down and went over to the sink. *That kids a pig*, Chuck thought. *He didn't even flush. Typical little boy for you though.* Josh did wash his hands and brush his teeth before leaving.

Another set of footsteps made their way up the stairs. As she paused at the top she said loudly, "Are you getting your pjs on Josh?"

"Yes Mom," Josh answered from behind his door. "Can I sleep in your room tonight? Just this once?"

Chuck could hear an exasperated parental sigh from Maria. "Now Josh, you know I'm not going to say yes. You're a big boy. We've been working on this." Josh continued for a minute or two with more cajoling, pleading, and guilt trips, but Maria was firm.

Then Josh pulled out the big guns. He began to cry. "But Mom, I'm scared because of the movie," he wailed. They were no doubt crocodile tears, but like any parent with a heart, Maria couldn't completely turn a blind eye to this ploy.

"Ok Josh, you can sleep in the hall outside my door, but you're not going to get a sticker on your chart for tonight."

Shit! I'm screwed, Chuck thought. *How the hell am I going to get out of here? I just need to calm down.* Chuck reminded himself to slow his breathing before he hyperventilated. Passing out in Maria's bathtub would definitely not earn him *Spy of The Year* honors if there were such a thing. *Wait. That's all I have to do. Wait. Maria and Josh will fall asleep. I'll tiptoe out of here and be on my way. The guys will just have to wait a bit longer.*

Chuck crouched in the darkened shower, trying to move as little as possible. The minutes passed painfully slow. He had no way to gauge the time except to look at his cell phone. That wouldn't do any good, and any unnecessary movement might cause a noise that would be heard. As he crouched, he began to feel a painful tightening in his left quadriceps muscle. *Shit, a muscle cramp*, he thought. He slowly eased himself upward, hoping to alleviate the increasingly painful knot in his leg. Chuck stood upright and shifted his feet ever so slightly to take the weight off his left leg, which was busy telling his brain that there were hot, sharp pokers in his thigh. As he shifted his feet, his left heel rested upon a tiny spot of shampoo that had not been rinsed away after Josh's last shower.

He felt his heel begin to slide and he reached out to grab the shower curtain to steady himself. *Ting!* The flimsy vinyl material snapped away from the little ring, which suspended it from above. *SHIT!* Chucks' brain screamed. *Ting, Ting, Ting!* One after the other, the little holes that held the curtains to the rings snapped away and Chuck felt his weight shift backward as his heel slipped forward on the spot of slick shampoo. *Ting! Ting! Ting!* Chuck flailed with his free hand and only managed to hit the faucet on his way down. Water poured into the tub as Chuck's ass hit the porcelain with the shower curtain on top of him.

"What the *hell* are you doing, Josh?" Maria shouted from the bedroom across the hall.

Chuck heaved himself out of the tub, flailing to get the shower curtain off him, and scrambled to his feet as light poured into the hallway from Maria's bedroom. He dashed into the hallway, leapt over the prone and confused Josh, and took the stairs two at a time as he hit the landing running. He caromed off the front door and headed through the kitchen, painfully clipping his hip on the island as he reached the back door. The door was locked and he fumbled with the deadbolt for a moment. Footsteps descended the stair as he flung the door open and jumped into the garage. He pulled the back door open, dashed across the backyard, and back into the darkness.

As he dove through the bushes and landed with a forward roll that took him to his feet on the other side, Schottzie began to bark again. He reached into his pocket and flung all of his remaining dog treats in the direction of the canine without slowing. He gave no thought to caution as he raced past Kirstner's house, around the pine tree, and literally leapt into the street in front of his car. He was *this* close to sliding across the hood like the Dukes of Hazzard. Unlike every horror movie he'd ever seen, Chuck easily grabbed his keys out of his pocket and quickly slid the key into the lock, hopped in, slammed the door, and roared off into the night. He could hear sirens beginning to build in the distance. They had to be for him. He couldn't imagine that Maria hadn't already called the cops. That was the problem with small towns. The cops never had enough to do.

Cooper

At the same time, I was leaving the playground empty handed with no dog and no beer. The teens stood in a small circle finishing their beers and watching me disappear into the dark path that brought me back to the neighborhood. Although my hands were empty, my mind was full. Full of the possibilities of what I had learned. My thoughts raced around my brain, bouncing off one another, colliding, answering some questions, but causing others. I lurked in the shadows of the trees, waiting for Chuck to return. The breeze whispered through the highest boughs, but the air around me felt almost oppressive in its stillness. The moon was just now peeking out from behind a high cloud. The midday shadows of earlier seemed to be hiding from me as well. The atmosphere as I stood among the trees was darker and colder, as if the forces of nature had turned their back on me, aware of what I had done, or perhaps turning a blind eye to what I must now face.

I paced nervously, trying to stay on the move, hopefully making it more difficult for the horde of tiny, buzzing vampires that circled my head from making a meal out of me. To stay here too long would risk discovery and possibly questions I couldn't answer. If the kids I had talked to were to exit the playground by this path and discover me still here, they would immediately be suspicious. *Where the hell is Chuck? What the hell is taking him so long?* My anxiety was relieved two minutes later as I saw headlights slowly making their way towards me. As before, Chuck extinguished the headlights as he entered the dead end and coasted to a quiet stop. I climbed in the passenger side and shut the door as quietly as possible.

"Damn! You smell nice! Did you get your hair done?" I found myself much funnier than everyone else did most days. It was great living in my little world.

"Shut up, asshole," Chuck grumbled. "You won't believe what I found."

Chuck shifted into reverse, executed a three-point turn, and we headed back to Goob's house, unaware that we would be waiting for friends who would never arrive. We both had shit-eating grins on our faces, certain that we had used our superior intelligence to gather the clues needed to solve this mystery. I sarcastically called Chuck "Matlock" and insisted he tell his tale first, eager to hold back my revelation so that I could have a grand unveiling, even if it was just for Chuck. We were both also unaware of the scene playing out on the playground I had so confidently left minutes ago.

The teens stood in a circle, looking expectantly in the direction of the far side of the playground where Goth Girl and Leader Boy had been searching for my dog. A shaggy-haired, skater-looking kid stepped from the line of trees and casually walked over to the threesome. He wore black sweatshirt, black jeans, and had a head of hair that almost covered his eyes and obscured his face. "So, do you think he bought it?" he asked.

Pimple Face eagerly spoke up, puffing out his chest as if hoping for approval from the new member of their group. "Oh yeah, he totally bought it. You can give the call. They'll be there."

24

On the one-minute ride back to Goob's house,

Chuck told me about finding the missing flash drive in Maria's house. Goob was going to be crushed. Since his divorce, he had been so down. I had been rooting for this to work out for him. Now it turns out that his new girlfriend is an evil cult bitch. Talk about your bad luck. Then again, as far as we could tell from his stories, his ex-wife had been an evil bitch too. She just hadn't found her cult yet.

We pulled into the driveway and both noted that the house was still dark. "Hmmm…that's weird," I said. You don't suppose that they're still out back on commando, do you?"

"They must be," Chuck replied. "Let's sneak up on them. C'mon." We may get old, but acting childish to annoy each other never does.

Chuck led the way as we took a circuitous route around the opposite side of the house and through the tall hedge so that we came out on the path behind them. We quietly crept up the path, trying to stifle our whispered giggles.

When we arrived at the back of the yard, behind the giant forsythia bush that was to be their cover, we both crouched low to look underneath. Our plan was to grab their feet and pull them out suddenly, hopefully scaring the hell out of them for a moment. Seeing nothing, our first reaction was disappointment at the fact that our joke would not come to fruition.

"Where do you think they are?" I said.

Chuck paused for a moment, rubbing his chin. "They either left to follow someone, or they went out for a beer. What do you think?"

"I think that if something was going on they'd have called or texted us. Those friggin' assholes went to O'Brien's and expected us to figure it out when we got here. They're probably drunk already."

We trudged up the path and around to the front of the house, still disappointed that the tables had been turned and they'd ended up surprising us. Then again, any of us showing up at O'Brien's for a beer is about as surprising as the sun setting every day. You know it's going to happen— it's just a matter of what time.

We walked into O'Brien's as if we owned the place, unaware that our arrival there had been observed with more than just the usual interest from our friend Seamus. O'Brien's was a small neighborhood bar that didn't try to be something it wasn't. There were no karaoke nights or 'ladies drink free' nights. To my sentimental heart, O'Brien's was the living embodiment of Cheers from the old TV series. The bartender and owner, Seamus, had inherited the place from his father about twenty years ago. Rather than pursue his dream of being a sportscaster, Seamus had listened to his mother, and his ingrained Irish-Catholic guilt, and had taken over the family business when his father passed away of a heart attack right there behind the bar. Seamus Sr.'s ashes were in a tarnished urn that sat in a place of honor on the shelf with the high-end liquors that no one ever ordered in a place like this. Then again, maybe they never ordered them because they were sitting with ashes. We didn't know and we didn't care. Although O'Brien's was located in a downstate New York suburb within an hour of New York City, Seamus and his father had never caved into the regions sports fans and they still proudly displayed their Notre Dame and Boston Celtics memorabilia throughout the bar. Rumor had it that Seamus had once physically escorted a patron out of the bar after he had jokingly implied that Larry Bird wasn't worthy of being in the Hall of Fame.

The waitresses and busboys changed with regularity, but Seamus and, occasionally, his now-aged mother, were the constants that made O'Brien's so comfortable for so many people. Broad faced and barrel-chested with dark, curly hair, Seamus was always quick with a joke about politics and a slap on the shoulder even if you weren't laughing with him. He was about ten years older than us and had always been kind of a surrogate big brother for our group, providing just the right words of wisdom minutes before closing time. Then again, by closing time, Winnie-the-Pooh would sound like brilliant philosophy to us. Maybe everyone didn't know my name when I walked in, but Seamus and Mrs. O'Brien did, and that was good enough for me.

"Well hello boys!" he shouted. "Only two of you tonight? Where are your partners in crime?"

Chuck and I looked at each other and burst out laughing at Seamus' choice of words while he could only stand there looking confused.

"Don't worry about it Seamus," I said. "We were hoping you could tell us. We thought they'd be here."

As he motioned to a barmaid to fill two mugs, he turned back to us and said, "Nope. Ain't seen'em tonight, although I'm sure they'll show up eventually. They always do, don't they?"

Chuck and I looked at each other with concern. This wasn't right. Goob and Cliff hadn't called, texted, and weren't anywhere we thought they would be. Something definitely wasn't right. We were all so cocky earlier when we had left with our master plan. We sat down and took our cold, frosty mugs from the barmaid. Of course, Chuck took a moment to try his best to charm her. Needless to say she was completely underwhelmed by his efforts to win her over.

Seamus finished up with a customer and walked down to our spot at the bar to chat a bit. Our discussion of the night's events and what to do about our missing friends would have to wait a few more minutes. As usual, Seamus wanted to talk about the Celtics and Red Sox and share neighborhood gossip about who had been in recently and what they'd said after a few-too-many drinks. He was always good for a laugh when he 'accidentally' let it slip what one of our mutual acquaintances had said or whom they had met with on the sly in a back booth. God knows what he might say to others about us when we weren't around.

"So Seamus, what's the good word this week? Anything new going on around here we should know about?" He shook his head and chuckled before regaling us with a story about a childhood friend of my sisters who had recently been charged with insurance fraud after a suspicious fire. Apparently her father had been in for Monday Night Football this week and had confided that he couldn't pay his tab because of his daughter's legal expenses. Then Seamus said something that caught our attention.

"Did some new folks move into the neighborhood? There are some new regulars hanging about here that I don't quite like the looks of. They look normal enough, but they just ain't friendly. They order their drinks and head to the back booths. They don't talk to nobody and they don't ever leave a tip. Assholes. I wouldn't mind if they took their business elsewhere."

Eventually he ran out of breath and had to stop talking. Generally, that was about the only thing that would stop his talking, but not for long. "One night after a few rounds I stopped by their booth just to check them out. I started a conversation by asking what they do and this is the weird part. One of 'em said he was a doctor over at St. Bernard's. He said it and just laughed as if he had said the funniest thing ever."

After Seamus went to tend to some new customers and left us to our beers, Chuck and I again reviewed our plan and what both of us had learned that night. "Are you sure?" Chuck said. "St. Bernard's Hospital? But that's been closed for a few years hasn't it?"

"Well," I replied, "between what Seamus said and what the kids told me, I think St. Bernard's is a place we need to check out."

What the teens at the school playground had told me was that there is indeed an Apocalypse Tribe hiding within our neighborhood, but that there's something else, something entirely more disturbing, going on, and the old, abandoned hospital is at the epicenter of it.

Josh, the kid who talked to me, didn't know exactly what was going on in the hospital building because he had never been invited to go there, but he was pretty sure that whatever it was, it wasn't good. He had told me that over the past ten years, three of his friends from the neighborhood had disappeared. He had been told the usual stories by their parents about them going to live with grandparents in another state or that they had been arrested for smoking pot and sent to 'juvie'. Josh didn't believe the stories because none of his friends had ever called or come back to the neighborhood, even once. He knew of some of the neighborhood adults who had supposedly taken jobs in other cities, or had died suddenly and unexpectedly, but he didn't care about that. He just figured that whatever happened to them was just a hazard of whatever they were doing. He didn't believe that any of the missing kids had any choice in what happened to them. He never seemed to have much choice in anything when his father put his foot down, and according to Josh, his father did it often and sometimes in ways that bordered on the abusive.

Josh acknowledged that he'd been hit before and that as a child he'd often been locked in his room for hours. Long enough that sometimes he had to pee out of his window or take a shit in his closet. The latter usually resulted in another cruel beating. Sometimes while he was in his room, his parents would forget about him and he'd hear them talking or arguing. That was when he had heard things that had made him scared of his father. More scared than any normal kid would be of any normally abusive father, if there were such a thing.

When the hospital had shut down, his father, an endocrinologist, had continued to leave for work every day as if nothing had changed. He no longer talked about his work much, but the hours seemed to be getting longer and longer. Josh's mother had presented a stoic front to Joshua. As a child, Joshua had noticed that this stoic facade seemed to be reserved for his father, but when it began to be presented to him on a daily basis, Josh had decided he'd keep his ears open and his mouth shut. He didn't want to disappear like some of his friends had done.

That was as much as I had gotten out of Joshua in the limited time we'd had to talk. He had seemed nervous and had kept looking in the direction of his friends on the other side of the playground. Josh hadn't struck me as a kid who could hold his beer or who could be particularly manipulative. He was just a scared, lonely boy who'd never had an adult in his life he could trust. Sometimes as adults we're a little too sure that we're smarter than kids. Because I was a children's therapist, my arrogance in this regard probably bordered on stupidity, but I just didn't know it yet.

25

Gooby

Gooby felt groggy, but he still knew who he was and had a vague recollection of how he had come to be where he was. Unfortunately, after someone had jabbed a needle in his thigh, he had no fucking idea where he was, but it felt like a coffin. A cold, metal coffin. *This is not good*, he thought. It was most definitely not good.

Unknown to even his closest friends, Gooby had claustrophobia. He had gone to great lengths and made a great many excuses to hide it from the rest of *The Golden Boys*. He was still not sure why he had hidden it all his life. The guys would surely give him the usual share of abuse, as they did about everything with each other, but in the end they would respect it and not lock him in closets or trunks too often. They all had their warts and most of the time the group either figured them out or they shared them with each other when they were really drunk.

As they'd gotten older, even if they didn't admit it, each of them had come to the sad realization that just maybe they weren't the immortal, invulnerable gods of youth that they had imagined they were. They realized that despite all their bluster and bravado when they were together, they were just ordinary men with the ordinary problems that all middle-aged men faced. No matter whom you are and how much you try to be Peter Pan, time has a slow, cruel way of reminding you that you're only human.

Unfortunately, Gooby wasn't feeling as if time were on his side. He had a few inches between his nose and the top of whatever box he had been stuffed into and he was laid out flat on his back. It was cold, but he could still breathe freely. His anxiety mounted as he considered whether or not that was just a temporary state of affairs. He wondered if the box that held him was airtight. Would he soon begin to gasp and labor for oxygen? If he were going to suffocate, would it be a painful struggle, thrashing helplessly about in what might well be his coffin? Or would he just become dizzy and lightheaded as if in a dream before passing into unconsciousness?

Gooby felt his heart racing as he contemplated his fate. His respirations were beginning to border on hyperventilation. He felt his fingers turn into claws, trying to dig into the smooth, cold metal that encased him. *I've got to relax,* he thought. *I'm not going to die. There's got to be a way out.* He had no idea how long he had lain unconscious. How long he had spent possibly using up what little oxygen was available without attempting to escape. *Even if I think of a way out, I might run out of air before I can do it. Do they guys even know where I am? Is there a chance they might rescue me? What if they never find me?* The questions seemed to be running laps around his mind. Gooby realized that his terror, his childhood nightmare, again had him in its terrible death grip.

He had been nine and was left home with his twelve-year-old brother while his parents went out for the evening with Cooper and Cliff's parents. It was the late '70s and their parents were still young adults who hadn't quite outgrown their partying days yet. They were probably at some cheesy dance club doing *The Hustle*, which passed for their generations' version of *The Macarena* or line dancing. Since his brother, Ricky, had turned twelve, he had managed to persuade his parents that he was responsible enough that he and Gooby didn't need to be babysat by Mary Ellen Watermelon anymore. Her name wasn't really Watermelon, but it rhymed and we were kids, so we thought it was funny no matter how many times we said it. Gooby figured that with his brother in charge he was in for a night of pre-pubescent decadence, which to him meant eating all the Fritos and ice cream in the house while they played hours of Pac Man until their parents got home.

Unfortunately, Ricky wasn't responsible enough to be looking after his little brother. He invited his friend Brian from down the street to come over while his parents were gone. Brian was the Eddie Haskell of the neighborhood. Or perhaps, more appropriately, had fate not intervened, the Ted Bundy of the neighborhood. He had a cruel, mean side that the parents of his friends never saw. Brian was the kid in the neighborhood who would viciously torture any stray, helpless animal that crossed his path, but moments later feign an Oscar-winning look of concern as he told old Mrs. Turnbaum that he hadn't seen her cat all day. He was the type of kid who was going to turn into a sociopath if the world didn't give him a serious ass kicking sometime soon.

As soon as Brian got there, he and Ricky literally shoved Gooby aside. "Get lost punk, we're playing the game now. Got to your room and play with your dolls." Gooby knew better than to try to cross his brother when he was outnumbered, and he was afraid of Brian.

Gooby muttered an "I'm telling Dad," and skulked away to his room. He and Ricky knew he'd never tell on him because Ricky was the one who had caught him and Chuck trying to smoke cigarettes out in the woods. Ricky had never told on Gooby about this, but continued to hold it over his head to ensure his own immunity from retribution by his younger brother. It was a reluctant alliance on Gooby's part and he was still at an age where he feared his parents' reaction more than he feared anything his brother could do to him. Gooby sat in his room reading his Spider-Man comics for an hour and a half until he got bored and hungry and decided to venture out of his room.

"Hey, what are you doing out of your room? We didn't say you could come out yet." It was Brian, and he had a malicious grin on his face and a tone in his voice that made Gooby very nervous.

"Let's get him!" Ricky and Brian dropped the game controllers and literally leapt up. Gooby was quick and had a couple steps on them. He raced down the hallway and into his room, slamming the door shut behind him. He leaned against it, praying that they had gotten their thrill in just scaring him, but his prayers went unanswered as both boys seemed to slam into the door behind him, knocking him forward so that he landed spread eagled and face down on the floor. He rolled over and looked up at the two older boys who had burst into the room.

He knew he could usually trust his brother not to take things too far, but when Brian was around he acted like a huge asshole. Brian quickly grabbed the blanket off the bed and threw it over Gooby, who was helpless to fight off the older, bigger boy. Gooby was quickly wrapped up so tightly in the blanket that he couldn't move—his arms and legs pinned to his sides as if he were in a cocoon. Brian was laughing like a hyena. A cruel, inhumane laugh. If he ever had the chance to see it, Gooby didn't think he'd be sorry if Brian got hit by a car. As Gooby lay helpless in the blanket, his eyes and mouth covered, someone delivered a punch to his gut that knocked the wind out of him, and a blow to his head that might have knocked him out if he wasn't wrapped in the blanket. He was dizzy, completely blinded, and he couldn't breathe. He felt himself being lifted, carried, and dropped like a sack of potatoes. It was only when he heard the closet door slam shut that he realized what had happened.

Gooby struggled and thrashed futilely against the blanket. He unable to see and labored to pull fresh air into his lungs through the scratchy, wool material. After a few minutes of thrashing about his panic had passed, but it was then that he had realized he had to pee, not just a little, but a lot. He held it as long as he could. The almost painful pressure from within his bladder was unbearable. Tears began to stream down his face. His sobbing cries for help were either unheard or ignored. They probably couldn't even hear him through the blanket, the closet, and the bedroom doors.

In the living room, the two older boys continued to play video games. They wrongly assumed that Gooby had freed himself but was just hiding in his room to avoid another beating. Eventually Gooby's bladder wasn't able to hold back the pressure and he had peed himself. Being only nine years old and exhausted from his struggles, Gooby fell asleep soon after.

A few hours later his parents had returned home, probably a little tipsy, and exchanged pleasantries with Brian, who headed home, and then took Ricky's word for it that his little brother had gone to bed. It was morning before Gooby was found and his gasping cries lasted for hours after he was released from the urine-soaked blanket. It started as a stupid, thoughtless prank and ended with Gooby forever sitting by doorways and avoiding crowded elevators. Now he imagined he could still hear Brian's cackling laughter outside of the metal box he was in.

His thoughts, as well as his pulse, were again becoming dizzying. *I have to get a hold of myself.* Despite the coolness of the air and steel around him, he could feel beads of sweat begin to grow on his forehead and upper lip. His breath was causing condensation to form on the polished horizontal surface inches from his face. *Great*, he thought. *It's going to be really pleasant when that starts to drip back down on my face, if I live that long.*

There was no room to bend his legs to push with his feet. He tried with his fingertips to grasp for whatever purchase he could get on the cold, smooth metal surrounding him, but it was to no avail. In frustration, he shouted and thrashed against the solid walls of what he was becoming more certain would be his final resting place.

27

"So what do you think we should do?" I asked Chuck. "Do we sit here waiting for Cliff and Goob, or do we assume something's wrong, head over to the old hospital, break in, and try to figure something out?" Chuck gave me that sheepish shrug of his shoulders he has had since he was a kid and took a swig of his beer. It was his way of answering anything he didn't have an answer to. His teachers and the three of us had grown accustomed to that look over the years, but damn it, he was *Spy Guy* now. I need a better answer than that. "C'mon Chuck," I said. "You're the big expert in this area. What do we do now? And don't you dare even try giving me that stupid shoulder shrug again. This is serious."

"The bottom line is, we can't just go breaking into an old hospital and wandering around. That place is too big for the two of us to search, and even though it's closed, they still keep security there for the offices in the attached professional building that's still open. They also need guards since the blood labs there are open 24/7 and to make sure that homeless people aren't trying to take up residence in the closed parts of the hospital."

He made sense, but it occurred to me that he seemed to know an awful lot about the security set up there. I was getting paranoid. Chuck couldn't be one of them, could he? He had lost his dad too. In fact, his dad was the first one of our group to die. At the time it seemed like your average, everyday heart attack. Then again, maybe that was a warning to Chuck to keep his mouth shut. I had known him since he was two years old. He couldn't be a member of a cult. Then again, his family had moved to our neighborhood. They weren't part of the original group that bought houses here before the lawns had grass and the streets had streetlights.

Shit, I was driving myself crazy. Everything had me rattled now. Then, using all the brilliant psychological weapons I had honed over the years, I came up with a plan that would hopefully unmask the truth.

Here I go, I thought. *It's now or never.* "So Chuck, how come you know so much about the security set up at St. Bernard's?"

Without a pause, or even a suspicious blink, he replied, "Remember five years ago when my mom passed away? She was treated at St. Bernard's. Sometimes when I was hanging around waiting for her appointments, I'd talk with the security guards. You know, just a professional interest I guess. It's kind of a habit. Wherever I go, I'm always checking out security, looking for loopholes. You never know where terrorists might choose to hide out or make a statement."

It sounded reasonable enough, I guess. I had for a minute forgotten to assimilate the new Chuck identity into my frame of reference for him. It sounded reasonable enough that it assuaged my anxiety of a few moments earlier anyway. I guess I did the same thing in a way. I was always checking people out psychologically, whether I was consciously thinking about it or not.

The barmaid, in response to a vague wave of the hand from Seamus, had come over, taken our mugs, topped off our beers, and returned them while we had been talking. Still no Gooby and Cliff though. Normally Chuck and I would be more than content to hang out at O'Brien's, playing darts and just passing the time waiting for our friends. Tonight wasn't 'normally' however. Although we had only been here about a half hour, I felt like mountains of time had passed us by as we sat there. Then she walked in.

"Hi guys!" We both turned at the same time, except I didn't choke on and then cough up my last swig of beer the way Chuck had. I burst out laughing. I couldn't help it. Regardless of circumstance, having your friend nearly snort beer out his nose is always funny. Fortunately, I wasn't drinking at the moment or I would have done the same.

Maria walked up and sat down on the barstool next to Chuck. She looked good in hip-hugger jeans and a sleeveless, black turtleneck, but her faced was flushed. I motioned to the barmaid for a beer to be brought to Maria. "You guys are not going to believe what happened tonight!"

Chuck and I eyed each other carefully, thus far successfully managing to maintain sober expressions. Maria took a quick sip of the beer and resumed talking rapid fire, spitting out the words like her mouth was an automatic weapon. She was obviously feeling a little high strung. "I had someone break into my house! Josh and I had just gotten home from the movies and we were going to bed when someone came bursting out of the bathroom and ran out of the house! The police came and took a report, but it took them nearly five minutes to get there. Whoever it was had to be a mile away by the time they arrived. I was so freaked out I couldn't bear to stay in the house. I took Josh to my friend Jessica's house—she has a little boy his age. They've known each other since they were in diapers. We're both staying over there tonight. She's watching the kids now. I just had to get out and have a beer to calm my nerves. Do you guys hang out here often?" She finally paused to catch her breath.

"Wow! That's amazing," I said. "Did you get a good look at the maniac?" I tried not to look at Chuck.

"No, he was down the stairs before I could figure out what was going on," she replied. "He pulled down the shower curtain in Josh's bathroom. Thank god he didn't hurt us. The police took a report, but nothing seems to be missing, so I doubt they'll do anything."

Chuck, still hoping to score points with Maria, put his hand on her arm lightly. "Well, I'm glad you're ok. If you decide to have a security system installed, I know someone that can do it on short notice."

Maria took a long swallow of her beer. "Thanks Chuck, I appreciate that. You smell nice. What is that?"

Chuck swallowed audibly, stammered a moment, and managed to spit out, "It must be my deodorant. I put some on just before I went out tonight."

'Hmm…" she said, "that smells almost just like Josh's shampoo."

At this point, I had to step into the conversation before Chuck's legendary lack of cool got us both arrested. "Anyway Maria, yes, we do hang out here a lot. In fact, and don't tell Seamus this, but we were getting served here for a year before we were even old enough. Do you come here very often?"

This time Maria paused, as if considering how to answer this question. "Oh, I've been here a couple times. Sometimes Jessica and I stop after work. Hey…umm…is Dave going to be coming?" She blushed a little and twirled her hair in her fingers as she said this.

Chuck saw it too and turned and rolled his eyes at me. He was just pathetic. I ignored him and answered

Maria, "I wish I knew. We've been waiting for him and Cliff. They were supposed to meet us here."

Now I started to hear the clock in my head continuing to tick and tock loudly like a metronome. For some reason I pictured an hourglass with the precious sands of time nearly gone. If Goob and Cliff had walked in, none of this would be worrying me, but they were still MIA as far as I could tell. I gave Chuck a look and said to Maria, "I'm sorry about what happened to you tonight, Maria, but Chuck and I have to get going. Normally we'd love to stay and keep you company, but we've been waiting for Cliff and Goob for too long already. We have to go find them."

It was then that Maria started to act suspicious. "Oh c'mon guys, can't you stay for one more beer? I'm all shook up and I'd love some company. Goob and Cliff are grown men. They can take care of themselves. I'll buy the next round."

Maria's speech suddenly seemed to accelerate again. She was talking the way she had when she had walked in. Quickly. *Too quickly*, I thought. *She's nervous and she's trying to stall us*. I could tell from Chuck's glance that he was thinking the same thing.

"Nope, sorry Maria," he said. "We've got to get going."

I threw a twenty on the bar and gave a wave to Seamus, who walked over to meet me at the end of the bar nearest the door. Without looking in Maria's direction, I quietly asked Seamus to keep an eye on her. I acted as if we were having a casual goodbye between friends with a clap on his shoulder and a handshake as we talked, but by the time we had walked out the door, Seamus understood that he was to watch for anyone who might walk in looking specifically to meet her. Being friends with the owner of the neighborhood bar had many benefits and, without any explanation needed, Seamus would call my cell phone if he saw anything interesting, or if Goob and Cliff showed up.

We quickly stepped outside before Maria tried some other ploy to slow us down. "So what do you..," I started, before Chuck cut me off.

"C'mon, let's get in the car," Chuck said. "We can stay low and keep an eye on the parking lot and on the door." We slipped into Chuck's Mustang, which he had backed into a parking space just so we could see the door or pull out quickly if we needed to. Apparently this was a habit of his carried over from his job that I had never noticed. Add that to the list of things I found out this week that I had missed when I wasn't paying attention over the last thirty years.

I was beginning to feel like there was the world you see and a whole other world hidden just beneath the surface. The existence of the cult, which had apparently been operating in my idyllic little neighborhood my whole life, our parents' involvement in some way, and Chuck's real job as a spy had completely taken me by surprise. That I had been blissfully unaware of all these things for years, suddenly made me feel very stupid, and very vulnerable. What else might I be missing that could possibly end up getting me killed? I was definitely not cut out for this line of work.

"So what do you think Maria was up to?" I continued. "Why was she trying to keep us there?"

"Well isn't it obvious?" Chuck said. "She totally wants me."

I burst out laughing. This was typical Chuck and I knew he was kidding, but I couldn't resist firing back. "Oh c'mon, we both know that's not true. She's a woman. When has a woman ever wanted you?" Chuck took this little bit of chiding as well as he usually does and returned to considering my question.

"Well, you're the psychologist. You read people for a living. What do you think?"

I wasn't prepared for the question to be turned back on me, but he was right. This was my area of expertise. I thought for a moment. "Well, there's two ways we could look at her behavior. First, we can assume that what she said is the truth. She might legitimately be shaken up because of the shampoo bandit who broke into her house, or we can think with our big heads instead of little ones and try to figure out why she would be trying to stall us. Considering the fact that you found Goob's flash drive in her house, we have to operate on the assumption that she can't be trusted."

"Hold on a sec," Chuck said. "We don't know for a fact that this is Goob's flash drive. We haven't actually put it in a computer and looked at it." He had that kinda hopeful look on his face that I recognized from the countless times in our lives when he tried to find the silver lining in a woman's subtle rejection. He had always been a sucker for the "we can still be friends" line. He actually believed it and tried to be friends with them. You can guess how well that worked out for him.

"C'mon Chuck," I said. "Remember, I said we're going to think with our big heads this time. You can't be serious."

Chuck was staring intently out the window at something and ignored my comment. "Hey Coop, do you see that gray Jeep over there?"

I nodded, waiting for him to continue.

"I noticed it when we came out. Look up at the top of the windshield, where the rear view mirror is. See that little red light that blinks about every ten seconds?"

"Yeah, what do you think it is?"

Chuck paused, as if in thought, then continued, "Well, I'm not sure, but I think there's someone in that truck watching us. Even though it's dark, I saw movement inside it. The little blinking light could be a camera and hopefully not a laser sight on someone's gun."

"Well, why don't we just leave," I said, "and see if they follow us? You can't catch a fish unless you cast your line."

Chuck turned his head to look directly at me. "You know what, Coop? That is a great idea."

Chuck turned the key and the powerful engine roared to life. He shifted in to gear smoothly and we rolled out of the parking spot and cruised right by the gray Jeep Cherokee. Both of us took great pains not to turn our heads, but to try to catch any possible movement inside the car with our peripheral vision. The windshield appeared as smooth and dark as a puddle of oil, giving no clue about its occupant, the darkness only broken for a fraction of a second by one tiny, red blink.

As Chuck pulled out into the road and slowly pressed down on the accelerator, I said, "You know, we could just be getting paranoid about Maria, the Jeep in the parking lot, Cliff and Goob missing, everything."

"I don't think so," Chuck replied. "Look behind us. I'm intentionally driving way too slow just so I could see if anyone is following us. They left the lot about three seconds after we did and then when they realized how slow I was going, they backed off. We've definitely got a tail."

Always the smartass, I said, "You're always looking to get some tail, Chuck, and *now* you've got a problem with it?" I turned my head to confirm what Chuck had said. "You're right though. They're back there."

I could see the color and make of the SUV each time they passed under a streetlight. When we stopped at a light they slowed to a crawl, ensuring that they wouldn't catch up to us before the light turned green. That was good—at least we weren't being aggressively pursued. In my mind I was picturing all those movie car chases where the passenger hangs out the window firing a gun, while the car careens recklessly at top speed. I'm not even sure Chuck knows how to careen. So far this seemed about as urgent and reckless as the O.J. chase.

"So what do we do now?" I said.

Chuck shrugged his shoulders. "I don't know. I'm usually the one doing the following."

"Well, then why don't you do what the people you follow usually do at this point?" And that's exactly what he did. Unfortunately, he didn't warn me that he was about to do it.

As soon as the light turned green, I heard Chuck's foot slam the accelerator to the floor and the rear tires squealed and burned as we took off. It almost felt like the Mustang was taking off right out from under us. If not for the headrest, I would have gotten whiplash. Chuck was definitely testing the advertised '0-60 mph' claim. After I had regained my equilibrium, I shouted, "Holy shit, Chuck! Give me a fucking warning next time!" I could still feel the force of the car's acceleration as we rocketed down the road. The wide, flat tires seemed stuck to the road as we careened recklessly around every bend.

Bracing myself, I risked a glance out of the rear window. It appeared that our friends from the bar had been caught off guard and were now trying to make up the gap. Chuck zigged and zagged through streets, turning unpredictably left and right. I could feel the beer I drank sloshing to and fro in my stomach. If this little joyride didn't stop soon, the beer would be going to and fro on the outside of my stomach and on the inside of the car.

The Mustang's engine revved as Chuck shifted gears up and down, expertly maneuvering the car through suburban streets that were definitely not designed with this kind of driving in mind. A slight crest in the road launched the car airborne briefly, like a scene out of Starsky and Hutch. We crashed back to the hard pavement without losing speed and the gray Jeep continued to follow us.

"Where are we going?" I shouted. Chuck ignored me, eyes intently on the road, occasionally flicking upward to glance at the rearview mirror. Our pursuers continued to dog us, matching us turn for turn. Just when we thought we might have lost them, they'd turn the corner behind us and accelerate.

Then Chuck surprised us all. As we hurtled down a small side street with the gray Jeep trailing us by about one-hundred yards, Chuck gritted his teeth and wrenched the steering wheel to the left, causing the Mustang to spin 180 degrees in a fraction of a second. My head was flung from one side to the other, bouncing painfully off the side window, stopping a moment after the car did. As the Mustang came to rest, Chuck immediately flipped the headlights off. We could hear the squeal of tires on asphalt as the gray Jeep came to a screeching halt about fifty yards away.

Both cars and their occupants appeared to be sizing each other up, unsure of what to do next. "What are we going to do next?" I asked. The engine was still idling, Chuck's foot lightly on the accelerator, and his hand on the stick. His cheeks were a little more red than usual.

"The last thing they expect," he said. His foot punched the accelerator to the floor again and we rocketed towards the Jeep. Due to the short distance between us, they only had a split second to consider their move, and this was what Chuck was counting on.

Inside the Jeep, the driver realized that if he didn't do something immediately, he would find himself in a very uncomfortable position. So he reacted. Nearly wrecking the transmission in his haste to throw the car into reverse and hit the gas, the driver turned his steering wheel and shoved it into reverse as quickly as he could think it. His only goal was to get out of the way of the large, black, metal object that was heading towards him a lot faster than he was comfortable with.

My hands went instinctively on the dash in front of me, bracing myself for what I was certain would be a horrific crash. The Jeep backed in an arc right into the ditch behind him as Chuck's Mustang clipped the front bumper, providing a little extra impetus in the right direction. We flew past, the gray Jeep just a blur. Then I heard raucous laughter from beside me. "Wooooo Hoooo! Ha Ha Ha Ha! I chickened that fucker right into the ditch! They can't even come after us now. That's right, who's the man? C'mon say it, Coop! You know it. I'm the man. Ha Ha Ha!" As we sped away, I risked turning my head to look out the rear window. Chuck was right. Our pursuers had indeed backed into a ditch and were helpless to follow us.

Chuck was obviously high on adrenalin, but he had a right to crow. I'm fairly certain I wouldn't have been able to pull that off. As we continued to speed down the street, still turning unpredictably in case there were others out looking for us, Chuck said, "C'mon Coop! Why so quiet? You didn't wet yourself over there, did you?"

Ignoring his childish attempt to gloat over his little victory, I said, "So what do we do now? They're probably already calling someone else, but right now we have the advantage since they don't know where we are or where we're going." Chuck thought for a moment, which in my opinion was a very long time for him. He continued to drive, but where to, I didn't know.

"Well, don't you think everything is pointing us towards the hospital? As long as we've got a minute, why don't you call Cliff and Goob? See where they're at. Maybe they can meet us there. Tell them to meet us in the staff parking garage. We can enter from the street side so that no one in the building will be able to see us, then we'll go in through the blood lab drop-off entrance in back."

I just looked at Chuck, my mouth no doubt agape, as I shook my head. "Where do you come up with this stuff?" I asked. "Do you just lie awake at night thinking about how to sneak into every building in the city?" He just laughed without taking his eyes off the road. "What the hell is wrong with you?" I said. "You need a hobby or a woman, and we both know finding a hobby would be easier for you."

"Why don't you call Goob?" Chuck said. "Put him on speaker. I changed his ring tone again. He hates when I do that."

"Oh no, what did you put this time?" I said. Chuck just laughed that stupid, cocky laugh of his. When this was all over I was pretty sure we were all going to kick his ass in some way, even if he did end up saving our lives.

28

Gooby

Gooby was concentrating on taking slow, deep breaths, hoping to keep the rising tide of panic at bay in his mind. Having been unconscious for god-knew-what amount of time and being completely engulfed in smothering, impenetrable darkness, he had no idea how long he had been...wherever he was. He cursed his own stupidity at having given up wearing a watch years ago. Always within arms' reach of a computer for most every day, he had no need to carry a timepiece. *I wonder where Cliff is,* he thought.

Then, with a vibration at his hip and a corresponding flash of light that was blindingly bright in the small, dark space he heard, *Connecticut's for fucking, that's all there is to do. I love to listen to classic rock and have sex with you.* Jesus H. Christ and the Four Hornsmen of the Apocalypse; one of those crazy bands only Chuck would know.

"What the fuck? I'm going to kill Chuck when I get out of here," he said aloud. *If I get out of here*, he thought inside his head. He struggled in the cramped space to get his hand to his cell phone and then to open it and move it up to his ear. *Connecticut's for fucking. It's the Nutmeg state. If we can't afford to buy antiques then we just copulate...*

"Hello... No, shut up. Listen to me. Someone ambushed Cliff and me. I'm stuck in a metal box of some kind somewhere. You've got to find me. It's like a coffin. I'm not sure how much air I have left in here."

Cooper

I was stunned. I couldn't believe what I was hearing. This wasn't possible. "Where's Cliff?"

"I don't know," Gooby said. We were under the bush behind the house and then I woke up here. This is totally not cool. You've *got* to find me!" He voice was strident and he sounded in a panic, as he well should. I was in a panic myself.

Then Chuck spoke up. "Tell him to calm down. Have him end the call with you, but keep his phone on."

"Goob listen," I said. "First off dude, you've gotta relax. If you keep talking like you're fourteen years old, we may just leave you in there. Secondly, Chuck's got an idea. I'm going to hang up now, but you leave your phone on."

Before he hung up, Goob said, "Tell Chuck he better not be the one to pull me out of here because I'm going to kick his ass for screwing with my phone again." Apparently Goob was still upset over the time he had flipped open his cell phone in a meeting, only to find that Chuck had changed his wallpaper to a picture of male genitalia. Thanks to a co-worker who had seen it over his shoulder, Goob was still living that one down at work. Imagine how pissed he'd be if he knew it was Chuck's genitalia. Yeah, we still haven't grown up.

We both did as he said and hung up. We had no better ideas and he was the only one that was keeping his head right now. "While I call the office and give them Goob's cell number, you try to call Cliff."

Chuck pulled the car over and called his office, giving them Goob's cell number and requesting a GPS trace. He said they'd call him back in a minute with Goob's location. At the same time I was dialing Cliff's number. If I got no answer, I'd know he was in trouble.

"Hey Coop! What's up? Where have you guys been?" Cliff sounded unusually chipper for someone who had supposedly been knocked out and kidnapped earlier.

"Umm…we're looking for you? Where are you?" Without

speaking and with eyes bulging, I frantically waved, gestured, and hit Chuck, trying to get him to understand that I had Cliff on the phone and that something was seriously wrong.

"Me and Goob got bored playing spy so we left. We're on our way to O'Brien's. Why don't you guys meet us there for a beer?"

I was beginning to hyperventilate. I wanted to scream, but at least this once I managed to keep my composure.

"Umm…yeah. We'll be there in a few minutes. We just stopped over at Chuck's so he could change." With a click I hung up and finally exhaled.

"Cliff is one of them," I said.

"What do you mean? How can he be one of them?" Chuck replied.

Taking a deep breath and speaking very deliberately, hoping my tone would help to make my point very clear, I said, "He said he was with Goob. He wanted us to meet them at O'Brien's." We both sat silently for a minute, pondering the sudden horrific revelation that one of our best friends may have murdered our fathers. Little did I know, Chuck was also pondering our next move.

Chuck and I both looked down. Chuck took a deep breath and exhaled in a quiet whistle. Then he picked up his cell and dialed again. "Yeah, it's me again. I need another 10-20. I'll wait on the line." He gave Cliff's cell number this time and waited. The minute it took for Chuck to get the answer he needed seemed an eternity as I sat there.

Again, I could sense the sands of time slipping through the hourglass that might just be measuring what life Gooby might have left. "Thanks, I owe you one. Later." Without a word, he put the Mustang into gear and accelerated smoothly into the street.

"Where are we going?" I said.

Staring straight ahead and gripping the wheel, he replied, "St. Bernard's. It's where they both are."

Compounding the sudden tension we both felt was a fog that had seemingly rolled in while we sat talking. Maybe we hadn't noticed it before, or maybe we had driven into it. This was a serious fog—thick as the proverbial pea soup. I had never told the guys this, but I was both fascinated by, and a little afraid of, fog. Damn that Stephen King! In his books, of which I have read far too many to count, there is always some menacing fog, often described with cool words like 'lugubrious', that usually precedes some blood sucking, soul stealing, or some other heinous act that gives my inner child nightmares.

I knew it was just moisture in the air, but to me fog at night seemed very menacing, almost malevolent. Definitely lugubrious. Like a living, moving thing it seemed to creep over the land. In the part of my mind that still held my child-like fears, I felt like the nighttime fog had stolen the daylight away and might never give it back. Tonight its thick vaporous tendrils appeared to be trying to blot out all the streetlights. This fog was the thickest I had seem in a long time. I had to remind myself to breathe. I know it's ridiculous, but when the fog is dense like this I feel afraid to breathe for fear that a lungful of the wet, murky air might smother me from within.

It was about a ten-minute drive to the hospital from where we were. I was thankful for the brief respite to gather my thoughts and take a few deep breaths. It just didn't seem right. It didn't correlate in my mind. Cliff had been our friend for over thirty years. We had known him since we were two.

Hmmm…that's it, I thought. *Since we were two…* I let the words, the idea, roll around my head for a while, waiting to see if it felt right when it settled into place. Remembering what I had read about *The Apocalypse Tribes* and their mysterious leader, Jeffrey Warren, I felt the puzzle pieces suddenly click neatly into place.

Jeffrey Warren and *The Apocalypse Tribes* had disappeared from public in the mid to late '70s, right around the time Cliff's family had moved into our neighborhood. Cliff's father was also mysteriously out of the country when both my dad and Gooby's dad died. *An alibi, or perhaps out of harm's way*, I thought. Either way, it just seemed too lucky, too convenient, and too suspicious not to be the explanation. I ran my theories by Chuck, who at first refused to even consider the possibility.

"No way," he protested. "Cliff is one of us. He's probably spent more time with us than his own family over the last thirty years. We would know if his family was in a cult."

But would we, I wondered. Recent evidence had certainly suggested that we were mistaken about our best friend, and about almost everything we had believed about our childhood. Based on what we had learned in the last five minutes, Chuck had to acknowledge that I was probably right.

It never occurred to us to wonder why Cliff had seemed to have the Midas touch when it came to almost everything. As I thought back to our childhood, I don't ever remember a time things hadn't been easy for Cliff. He always got the girl, got the grades, and scored the touchdown. Looking back, it all seemed too perfect.

I know every town has their high school heroes, but usually when they make the jump from being a big fish in a small pond, they find out that in the big pond they're as likely to get eaten as anyone else. Cliff had seemed to make the jump to the big pond effortlessly. Until his tragic knee injury, he looked to be on the fast track to college sports stardom. Following his knee rehab, he studied to become a physical therapist and, by all accounts, his practice was thriving. It had become a mecca for professional athletes rehabbing their own injuries. Again, I thought, *Cliff's success seems too uncanny and too easy. Could the Apocalypse Tribe have something to do with it?*

Shit. "I wish I had the Internet available," I said. The fog was interfering with my cell signal. It occurred to me that despite the familiarity of the name Jeffrey Warren, I had never seen a picture. Right now I'd love to know what he looked like. Cliff certainly hadn't gotten his good looks because he was in a cult, unless *The Apocalypse Tribes* were into genetic engineering. Then again, Cliff did look like Adolph Hitler's wet dream. But right now, I wasn't wondering how much Cliff resembled Jeffrey Warren, at least not directly.

Despite the coincidence of when he moved to our neighborhood, Chuck and I couldn't think of a single incident of suspicious behavior from Cliff in our entire lives. If he wasn't part of the cult, then why was his dad the only one still alive? Why was his dad suddenly safely out of town when all the shit hit the fan this week? Why was Cliff lying to us about his whereabouts? Why was I using words like 'whereabouts'? Nobody talks like that outside of the stereotypical TV cops. At least I had the good sense to filter pretentious crap like that out of my everyday conversations.

I was abruptly reminded that my suddenly insightful musings weren't worth a rat's ass at the moment when Chuck said, "We're almost there. You ready?" We had both been quiet during the ride. Chuck had been quietly plotting our entrance to the hospital and formulating a search plan while I had been wasting my time trying to fathom the turn of events that had been forced upon us this week.

29

Cliff

As Cliff walked into O'Brien's, he was greeted by Seamus, who informed him that he had missed Chuck and I just a little while earlier, but he didn't know where we had gone. After exchanging pleasantries with Seamus for a minute, Cliff was turning to leave when he heard, "Cliff! Is that you? Come here, sit down with me!" It was Maria, still nursing her beer and waiting for a companion. She told him the story of her terrifying encounter with the intruder in her house. Cliff impatiently glanced at his watch and listened as sympathetically as he could while she rattled off her story again, rapid-fire and without pause. "You know, I never noticed it before, but you guys all dress alike. Cooper and Chuck were in black too," she said as she finally stopped to take a breath.

"Speaking of Cooper and Chuck," Cliff said, "I've really got to get going to find them. Don't worry—Chuck will use his contacts to hook you up with a good security company tomorrow. Have a nice night."

As Cliff rose and began to turn towards the door, he felt her hand on his forearm. "Are you sure you can't stay for a beer? I'm buying." Her brown eyes made contact with his and she smiled demurely.

Is she coming on to me? Cliff thought to himself. *She can't be. She's into Gooby. Why is she trying to keep me from going? Well, I suppose it can't hurt to stay for just a beer. Maybe I'll find out something useful,* he rationalized.

Although he was married, Cliff was never one to turn his back on a pretty face. He would never cheat on his wife, but as he headed full steam for middle age, the attention of an attractive woman helped make him feel a little less like an old, married guy. It was true for all of us.

Cooper

Admittedly, Cliff and I lived a few thrills vicariously by hanging on every detail we could get from Goob and Chuck about their 'glamorous' single lives. I'm not sure which was more pathetic though, Chuck and Goob's' dating lives or mine and Cliff's envy of them. As they say, the grass is always greener on the other side. Goob and Chuck were dating in hopes of settling down happily and securely like we had. Two single and two married. It was a nice balance for our little group. I suppose if everyone settled down and had kids we truly would grow into the middle-aged men we still didn't believe we were.

Cliff

There was no doubt about it. Maria was flirtatious, and as much as Cliff was enjoying her company, he would never accept any kind of invitation from her. Even if Chuck had called it that first night on the street, Goob had dibs. It was the *Guy Code*. We never spelled it out, but we all lived by it. Sometime, when I'm done with my next great psychology book, I'll have to sit down and write a book about the *Guy Code*.

Cliff enjoyed his beer and Maria seemed to be enjoying his stories about the athletic exploits of his youth until, from out of the blue, Maria said, "Wait a minute, where is Dave? Chuck and Cooper said he was with you."

Cliff stammered, almost choking and spitting out his beer before recovering. "You know, that's a good question, and another reason I've got to get going. I think I might know where Cooper and Chuck are. I hope Goob is with them."

This time as Cliff rose from his seat to go, Maria stood up as well. "Well, if I've got no company I might as well get going too."

She began to rummage in her purse when Cliff said, "Don't worry about it. I've got it," as he gave a nod to the barmaid and threw a twenty on the bar.

30

Cooper

Although it is generally a shelter from the weather, the entrances and sides of the parking garage were open. Tonight the fog seemed to be slithering into the garage of its own volition, like a snake extending its tongue to sniff for prey. Until Chuck and I arrived, the garage appeared to be devoid of prey for the fog or anyone else. Over the past week we had pretty much just reacted to everything happening to us, but tonight we had gone looking for trouble and found more than we'd ever imagined. I felt like we were walking into the lion's den. I was afraid to even whisper inside the car for fear that I would trigger some sort of alarm that would have us instantly surrounded by black-masked, gun-toting thugs. I really did not want to finish my night dead.

Chuck decided to forego a turn signal as we pulled off the street and he extinguished the headlights before we entered the garage. In keeping with the whole 'going out of business' motif the hospital had been working on, there were no lights on anywhere in the parking garage. I assumed that they turned out the lights at a predetermined time every night as a cost-saving measure. Regardless of the reason, the darkness and fog made it feel as if we were driving into a mausoleum or modern day catacomb. The only sound was the engine echoing off the cold, dark cement walls.

"Why don't you park here?"

"No, we can't leave it on the first floor. It would be too easy for someone to spot from the street or the hospital," Chuck replied. "Shit. I wish I had one of my sets of night-vision goggles. Cliff and Good better not have lost them when they were busy getting kidnapped. I really don't want to have the cost of those coming out of my pay."

And so we continued upward, following the angular corkscrew pattern that the garage was laid out in. The muted light that filtered in from the outside was all Chuck had to use to guide his way. If there was another car parked in our path, we would surely run into it. Finally, at the third level, Chuck stopped the car. The parking garage was six-levels high, but cement barriers prevented us from going further, now blocked the ascending path.

"What do we do now?" I asked. Chuck paused, eyeing the barriers. The powerful engine of the Mustang continued its deep, rhythmic rumbling. We could certainly climb over the barriers if we needed to, they were only about three feet high, but going further in the car was definitely out of the question. "This is far enough," he replied. "We just needed to be able to park the car where it wouldn't easily be seen. C'mon."

He said it so casually, as if we were just hopping out of the car to go into the mall. If he was nervous, he didn't show it. At the moment, I was feeling anything but casual. I was scared shitless. I hoped that it didn't show. I wanted to be as cool as the awesome crime-fighting spies we pretended to be as kids. Taking a deep breath, I opened my door and stepped out of the car. Out of habit, I threw the door shut as I normally would. Chuck jumped and looked at me as if he had been shocked with electricity. He looked like he was about to chastise me for having been so careless when his open mouth was abruptly shut by another noise.

The noise came from one of the levels below us. It sounded like several metal-link garage doors dropping down from the ceiling and slamming to the hard concrete floor. As far as I knew, the parking garage only had two exits with an entry and exit door at each one—avenues of escape that I now assumed were blocked. We were trapped. I suddenly felt like one of those stupid cartoon characters that walk right under the box propped up on a stick to sniff the cheese. Unfortunately, it wasn't Bugs Bunny, or even Wile E. Coyote who had pulled out the stick.

"Coop! You idiot! Why did you slam your door?" Chuck shouted.

"Shhhhh! Geez! Stop yelling!" I tried to shout-whisper back at him. The shout-whisper never works, does it? We all hear it no matter how discreetly someone tries to do it, and yet we all continue to use this pathetic attempt to maintain some sense of privacy or decorum.

"Knock it off, Coop! It doesn't matter. They know we're here now," he again shouted as he walked around to the trunk of the car and proceeded to unlock it. From within, he grabbed a rectangular, smooth, black metal case that was thicker than a briefcase, but about the same dimensions in length and width. With another small key he quickly opened this, revealing two handguns nestled safely in their own cut-out spots in the gray foam inside the case. "Here, take this," he said, handing me one of the weapons.

I'd love to tell you what kind of gun it was, but I have no idea and I was too freaked out at the time to consider asking. It could have been a .350 Magnum, a .351 Magnum, a .352 Magnum, or an AK47 or 48 for that matter. I knew what I knew about guns from television. I also knew they could kill. I knew that from firsthand experience. It turned my stomach the way it had twenty-five years ago when I had seen up close what a gun could do to a person.

I had been thirteen years old and, like most kids, I still held the belief that the future could hold greatness for me. I was a runner, as most of my family was. We were not joggers as most people say. In my mind, joggers just plod along at a nearly sedentary pace that makes me look around to see if there's a hare racing ahead to a finish line somewhere. At the time, I thought I was the hare. During the summer months I would train on the roads every day, running miles and miles alone, getting stronger and faster. I had dreams of a future filled with Olympic medals and the front of a Wheaties box.

Who knows, maybe that could have been in my future, but in all honesty I ran because I was good at it, not because I loved it. Without a love for it, I didn't have the drive, the single-mindedness to train hard enough to be great. It's one of the great 'what-ifs' in my life. Don't we all have one of those? We're all talented enough at something, but sometimes when we reach the fork in the road too many of us don't recognize the opportunity and we take the path of least resistance or the path to immediate gratification.

So that hot, humid summer day all those years ago when I hadn't come to my fork in the road yet, I was running down another long, lonely road. South Bay Road, I believe it was called. It was a fairly rural area with little traffic and only occasional houses or farms. It was the kind of hot summer day when the air is heavy and still and the only sound is the constant chattering of the crickets. It was summer vacation, and with both my parents working, I pretty much took care of myself during the days.

As I ran along the quiet, two-lane road, imagining myself pounding the pavement towards future glory, up ahead and on the opposite side of the road I noticed a car that looked as if it had sort of dived head first into the trees and brush that crowded the road closely here. It was a brown sedan of some sort. The kind you swear you'll never drive but always end up with by the time you're forty. It was still and quiet. There was no movement apparent inside or outside the car. It could have been there five minutes or five days for all I knew.

The heat and monotony of my long run encouraged me to take a quick breather, just to make sure no one was there. I slowed to a jog, and unnecessarily looking both ways, crossed towards the sedan. There wasn't much of a ditch at all, so it could be easily backed out of the bushes when someone chose too. Perhaps the driver had wandered down the road in search of help. As I approached the car, I first noticed the smell, and then I noticed the window.

The smell was a fresh, wet smell, the kind that registers fleetingly in your nostrils as your car speeds by a recent bit of road kill. The smell didn't overwhelm me. Out on these old country roads there were often unpleasant smells emanating from the nearby bogs or farms. As I cautiously approached the car, expecting to find nothing of interest and planning to continue on my way momentarily, I saw the driver's side window.

To me it looked as if someone had thrown a basketball covered in red paint against the window. There was a large circular area as if something had hit the window and bounced off. Rivulets of reddish, orange liquid seemed to be racing for the bottom as if they couldn't escape quickly enough. The little rivers of what I now feared was blood were still moving, telling me that whatever had happened had happened within minutes of me coming by. I ran the last few steps to the car window and peered inside past, through the red explosion on the window. Inside, laid across the seat, was a man with a pulp of blonde hair, blood, and bits of bone where the side of his face should have been. In his right hand, which lay on the seat stretched above him, was a gun.

I turned away and leaning forward, vomited what little was in my stomach onto the toes of my shoes. As I felt the yellow liquid begin to seep through my socks, I sat down by the side of the road, feeling dizzy. It seemed like an eternity, but was probably only a minute or two before another car came by and stopped. The old lady inside was horrified by what she saw there, but had her wits about her enough to lead me into her car and drive to her house just down the road to call the police.

I later learned from news reports that the man had been an off-duty state trooper who had for some unknown reason, chosen that day, that moment, to commit suicide as he drove down South Bay Rd. towards me. As quiet as the day was, I hadn't heard the shot inside the car and was unlucky enough to come along only minutes after it happened. To this day, my stomach still turns at the sight of a gun and the image I can't get out of my memory of that man's brains splattered on the window as if a paint-covered basketball had been thrown there.

As I held the gun Chuck had handed me, I could feel my stomach lurching inside. I had never held a real gun before and the fact that I was holding one now scared me. If I had to, I wondered, could I make someone's brains splatter like the state trooper had his own? Could I really do that to another human being? I hoped I wouldn't have to find out.

It was solid, heavy, and cold in my hand. It felt powerful and dangerous. I wasn't sure I could handle it if I had to. I knew what people in movies looked like handling a gun like this, but who's to say that's what works in real life?

As a kid, Goob's family and mine shared Thanksgiving dinner every year, and every year Goob and I had our own tradition. Long before I had found the dead state trooper, we would take out my Red Ryder B.B. gun— yes—just like the one Ralphie had gotten in *A Christmas Story* and pretend to hunt in the woods and fields behind my house. No one told me I'd shoot my eye out and frankly, my marksmanship skills were so poor I doubt I could have done so even if that were my intent. We always hoped to hit a bird, squirrel, or rabbit, but never did. That was the extent of my previous gun toting experiences. I hoped that growing up automatically made you a better marksman or I was screwed here.

From the case my gun had come from, Chuck took a round, smooth cylinder of metal about three inches long and screwed it tightly into place on the barrel of my gun. *A silencer*, I thought. I knew this from television. He then checked each ammunition clip and snapped them smartly back into place. He continued to rummage through similar sleek, black lock boxes in his trunk. His movements in handling the guns and in everything else were smooth and efficient—as if these were actions he had done a thousand times before. He opened one box that contained ammunition clips and slipped one into each of his pockets. "Hey, why don't I get any?" I protested.

"Coop, there's one clip already in the gun. If you use that up, I may have to shoot you myself. Shut your mouth and follow me, and if you've got any balls at all, now might be a good time to take them out."

Chuck was SO going to get his ass kicked when this was all over. In typical *Golden Boy* fashion, whenever one of us gets a little too cocky, the rest of us take it upon ourselves to knock them down a few pegs by getting the offender drunk and embarrassing him in a very public way. Generally we don't need much help embarrassing ourselves when we're drunk; we just need a push in the right direction.

It's too bad that women couldn't see Chuck the way he is when he's playing *Spy Guy*. They'd be totally into his calm, cool nerves-of-steel act. But, like most of us, no matter how confident we are, a pretty smile and some well-placed curves turn our brains to jelly.

I decided that I'd plan my pre-pubescent vengeance later and follow Chuck's lead for the time being. What other choice did I have? I sure as hell hoped Chuck knew what we we're going to do because it was a very unsettling feeling, to say the least, to be trapped in a dark parking garage three floors up with no way to escape. Rather than making me feel more secure, the gun had the opposite effect. I didn't relish the thought of being in a situation where I'd have to fire it at another human being, but my self-preservation instinct was strong enough that I think I could do it. At that moment, any reservations I might have about killing another person went out the window when I reminded myself of what brought me here—the sight of my fathers' body lying in a puddle of blood and sawdust on the basement floor of my childhood home.

The garage remained utterly silent and still. The streetlights outside were muted by the thick fog, giving us almost no illumination as we crept along the concrete wall towards the side of the garage that faced the hospital. Still dressed in the black outfits we had donned to start this night, we would be very difficult to spot. We had to get into the hospital, Gooby's life might depend on it, but first we had to find a way out of the giant concrete and steel cage we had driven right into.

Chuck moved forward stealthily along the wall with me in tow. The aisle was gradually inclining upward as we approached the corner where it turned to go up to the next level. I didn't feel like I was as smooth at creeping around as Chuck was, but I thought I pulled it off pretty well. After all, this was what we had played at all those summer nights years ago when we patrolled the neighborhood. Chuck motioned for me to follow him as he lowered himself and skittered almost crab-like across the aisle to the side where the garage had long, rectangular openings that faced the hospital.

We crouched beneath the level of the window as Chuck listened for any sound from below. There was none. The silence felt almost deafening, heavy. If they knew we were here, why weren't they just barreling up here with guns a blazing to take us out? The fact that they hadn't immediately come after us put me on edge. The locked lower levels and the silence gave me the impression that we were being toyed with—that they were in control and just taking their time deciding when they would get to us. *This was taking too long*, I thought. We had to get inside and find Gooby.

As Chuck turned to look over the ledge at the hospital, the waistband of his underwear peeked out from the gap between his jeans and his shirt. The clod was still wearing tighty-whities! I seriously gave thought to giving him a wedgie to break the tension but reconsidered when I reminded myself he was holding a loaded gun. *I'll get him later when he puts his gun away*, I thought to myself.

31

As I sat there, feeling like a sitting duck, I realized that this was a chess game. They make a move, we make a move. Unfortunately, it was a chess game we had been losing badly so far. Our moves had been reactions to their moves. They were controlling us. We had been toyed with. They had let us stay in the game like a cat that lets the wounded mouse run a bit before slashing at it again with its razor-sharp claws.

We had been playing Blindfold Chess up until now. They could see the board but we were in the dark, not even knowing the game existed. Heading into the hospital was our first aggressive move that they hadn't provoked. In chess terminology, Chuck and I appeared to be a 'desperado piece', determined to sacrifice ourselves—but we weren't playing for a stalemate here. They wouldn't let us just stay in the game anymore. By marching our king right onto their side of the board, we had begun the endgame with a fatal checkmate as the only possible outcome.

Not having the time to seriously pursue my passion for chess the way I'd like to, I often found myself in local tournaments competing against seasoned players who often travel the country participating in tournaments to gain points and improve their rank within the U.S. Chess Federation. Although I was usually outclassed, I was not without my own skills. On occasion, I could surprise a highly ranked and overly smug opponent with a 'swindle'—a clever play in which a player in a losing position tricks his opponent, perhaps by playing possum a bit, and thereby snatches victory from the seemingly certain jaws of defeat. It was considered a cheap victory by the better players, but I wasn't proud. I'd take what I could get. To get out of here alive, Chuck and I were going to have to swindle our asses off.

The Apocalypse Tribe had seemed fairly confident in their ability to get away with murder so far and I was hoping that their arrogance would make them ripe for a swindle. If they underestimated the danger of allowing us to walk straight into their lair, then we might be able to bring them down. The problem is, I didn't have a plan and it still felt like they were in control. In chess I'm typically thinking several moves ahead, but here I had no way of anticipating their moves or planning my responses. No way of predicting how I might goad them into a misstep. Then again, their false sense of security in their ability to control and direct us into their trap could work to our advantage.

That could be our advantage, I thought. We needed to behave in an unpredictable manner to push them into a quick, poorly thought out reaction that would give us the upper hand. The seconds were ticking away as we sat there, crouching in the dark, damp parking garage. Gooby's seconds might be ticking away, and our advantage, any element of surprise that Chuck and I had, might be ticking away as well. We needed to move quickly to keep them off balance.

Then we heard it. It wasn't the last thing we were expecting, but it was still unsettling and completely threw me off balance. "Hey guys! Where are you? It's me, Cliff! I want to help." Chuck and I looked at each other as his voice echoed through the empty garage. Because of the impeccable acoustics in the garage and the slight muffling of sound due to the fog, we had no idea if his voice was coming from above or below. "Warriors, come out and play!" he shouted in the familiar sing-song manner we knew from our youth. He was quoting an old gang movie from when we were kids. The leader of one gang had led his group through the streets at night shouting this line, trying to goad their enemies into challenging them. It had been funny to walk around the neighborhood at night in our little gang shouting this line to our friends. Cliff was obviously trying to use humor to get us to let down our guard, but here, in these circumstances, it suddenly sounded more menacing than humorous. "Guys, c'mon, I can get you out of here. You don't think I'm working with them, do you? Come on out."

We looked at each other and rolled our eyes as if to say, "Fuck. Now we know he's working for them." Sometimes there's nothing like the f-bomb for expressing exactly how you feel at that moment.

After thirty years of friendship, we didn't need to say much to understand what each other was thinking. We know every facial expression, gesture, and every nuance of each other's tone of voice. Whether it be in a loud bar trying to hook Chuck up with women, or in a parking garage being stalked by our former best friend, we knew each other so well that usually only a look or a single word was needed to convey an idea. I knew what we were both thinking at that moment. Neither Chuck nor I wanted to be put into a position where we had to shoot Cliff. He may have betrayed us, but we had literally lived our lives with him for the last thirty years. Not everything we shared could have been an act. In order to avoid that possibility, we were going to have to get out of this garage without confronting him.

We didn't know if it was safe to go up or down. Hell, it might not be safe either way. We likely didn't have time to get back to our car, and what would we do if we did? There was also nowhere to hide. A parking garage is a barren, ugly place when it's empty, appearing to be as gray, cold, and empty as the surface of the moon. I leaned forward and glanced out of the garage towards the hospital. We were three floors up and we had to get out. Then I saw our chance. As I turned to whisper to Chuck, an engine roared to life and we heard the squeal of tires. "Follow me!" I shouted to Chuck and then took off running along the wall. As we passed the corner I saw headlights light up the wall behind us. *C'mon...almost there*, I thought to myself. Chuck had obeyed my directive and was right behind me. The headlights continued to race along the wall just behind us.

With any luck, we hadn't been seen yet. My legs pumped furiously, my feet pounding the ground faster than I had run since high school. As I reached my goal I glanced over my shoulder, briefly making eye contact with Chuck and grabbing the ledge, I vaulted out the side of the parking garage. As I dropped below the opening, I could see Chuck's eyes get a little crazy for a split second before he realized what I was doing. Then he too vaulted out into space three stories above the ground.

My feet hit the roof of the elevated walkway that connected the garage to the hospital and I tumbled forward, briefly teetering dangerously near the edge before rolling to a stop. Chuck hit right behind me and fell on top of me in a heap. "Why Chuck, I hardly think this is the time, and besides, I'm married. You should be ashamed of yourself," I said as I tried to catch my breath. Chuck, as usual, rolled his eyes at me.

The walkway between the parking garage and the hospital was about one hundred feet long and entirely enclosed. It was about eight feet across and flat on top where we had landed. "Man that was a nice move. You think they saw us?"

I shook my head. "We'd be filled with bullets by now if they had, but we don't have long before they figure this out. We have to find a way into the hospital from here." I was hoping the thick fog would obscure us from view if anyone looked out of the hospital or garage, but hoping for luck like that would only get us killed.

"You know what?" Chuck said. "They know we're here and they know they lost us, so it's only a matter of seconds before they come after us full force. If we stay here we might as well be target practice for them. Follow me." Before I could protest or ask for an explanation, Chuck stepped around me and began to run atop the enclosed walkway towards the hospital wall. He disappeared into the fog, turning into a shadow that quickly began to recede from me. I could hear his footsteps and began to run after them. One slip in this fog, one wrong step, could send me tumbling thirty feet to the ground. I concentrated on running in as straight a line as possible. My feet skidded to a halt as I almost ran right into Chuck, who had stopped short of the hospital wall. I briefly flailed my arms to regain my balance and grabbed a hold of Chuck's arm to steady myself.

The hospital loomed above us. The walkway we stood on entered on the second floor and ten more stories stood above us. In its time this had been the largest hospital in the tri-state area, but now it was a sad, empty monolith. A testament to the passage of time, the advancement of modern medicine, and the business it had become. What it also may be is our final resting place. Something had to give tonight. The envelope had been pushed and with our actions we had chosen to, as poker players say, go all in.

Did Chuck think we were going to go all Spider-Man and scale the wall to the roof? In the movies there was always an entrance on the roof of every building. We certainly couldn't jump down from where we were. Then Chuck did the last thing I expected. Well, ok, not the last thing, because in general Chuck usually does a lot of things we don't expect. The only difference was that this time he was sober and there was no woman here to throw a drink in his face and storm off.

Chuck drew his gun and laid flat on his chest at the very edge, hanging his arm, and the hand holding the gun, over the edge. "Here goes," he said, just before I heard his gun fire. It wasn't the sound of his silenced gun that surprised me. It was the sound of the glass wall of the walkway beneath us caving inward that seemed to erupt into the quiet night. "Follow me," Chuck shouted. He knelt, grabbed the edge of the roof, and jumped, using the leverage of his hands to swing himself into the opening beneath us that he had just created. As certain as a bullhorn, Chuck's shot had announced our presence. I had the blink of an eye to trust him and follow his lead this time. He was *Spy Guy* after all. Who was I to argue?

I swung in, landed awkwardly, and tumbled to a stop amid the pile of shattered glass. Chuck was already standing up and reached down to take my hand and help me to my feet. I had cut my hand pretty badly when I hit the floor and winced as he pulled me up. Blood covered both our hands and Chuck nonchalantly wiped his hand off on his pant leg. "C'mon," he said. His calm demeanor was unsettling.

Inside my head there were competing voices. Not the "I need thorazine" type voices, but the voice of my conscience arguing with itself. My inner child was shouting, *WooHoo! This is awesome*, while my logical adult voice was screaming, *No! Make it stop! I can't do this!* Unfortunately I didn't have much choice right now, so I chose to ride shotgun with my inner child. I ran after Chuck with the sound of glass crunching beneath my feet.

We entered a large, open atrium area with an abandoned information desk, a chained café entrance, and hallways going off in every direction like the spokes of a bicycle wheel. Each hallway had a colored sign above it with a number and on the floor of each hallway in the same color was painted a one-inch wide line that stretched from the information desk down each hall to the end. I remembered this system from the few times I had to come to the hospital to visit friends or to see a specialist. I always felt like I was a kindergartner when the aide at the reception desk said something like "Follow the red line down this hallway until it intersects with the yellow and then follow that to the end." It was a ridiculous method of giving directions to adults, but it worked. I'd subsequently find myself walking for several minutes without once looking up as I obediently followed the stripe on the floor. Needless to say that although it got people where they were going, it occasionally resulted in a few head on collisions.

Chuck hesitated for a second before dashing into the green hallway nearest on the right with me on his heels. We ran full speed down the darkened hallway. What little light there was from the atrium we had just left was fading fast as we moved further away from it. We would soon be immersed in total darkness. Ahead of me, Chuck slowed to a halt before a pair of double doors. Because of the poor lighting and how fast I was running I plowed right into Chuck, giving myself a mouthful of his hair and an intimate appreciation for the amount of time he had obviously been spending on the Stairmaster. "Nice glutes, Chuck," I said. "Where to now?" I didn't have to see his face to hear the exasperated sigh and know that he was rolling his eyes, *again*. Sometimes my near-constant inane banter drove my friends crazy, but it was what I used to cope with the world, and if this wasn't a situation that required some massive coping, then I don't know what is.

"C'mon," Chuck simply said before he carefully and quietly pushed through the double doors that indicated an entrance to an old unit of some type. On the right was the nurses' station, complete with an empty coffee mug, pens, clipboards, and papers strewn carelessly about. The board on the wall behind the nurse's desk still listed room numbers, names, and medication times, as if the hospital had simply been abandoned in the middle of a busy day. Ahead was a gloomy hallway with what appeared to be patient rooms lining both sides. After the chaos of the last two minutes, the eerie quiet of the empty unit should have been a relief—but it wasn't. It felt ominous and threatening. I always found it strange to be in a very busy place when it's empty. Like driving city streets in the very early morning hours or being alone on a subway, it felt as if something sinister had occurred to wipe out the rest of the human race when I wasn't looking. I found the empty hospital similarly creepy. I had only ever seen this place when it was full of the non-stop hustle and bustle of people in every hallway on their way to some definite destination. It just felt wrong somehow.

We knew we couldn't go back, but we also didn't know if there was a way out. Just as I was about to suggest to Chuck that we turn back so that we weren't trapped in a dead end hallway, the gloom lifted a bit. From behind us, the hallway we had just come from lit up with the feeble light provided by the backup emergency lights that were affixed near the ceiling every twenty feet or so. A tide of panic began to rise quickly in my mind as I realized that they knew where we were and turning back was no longer an option.

33
Gooby

As Gooby lay there, he felt himself getting lightheaded. *Is this real, am I starting to suffocate?* he wondered. *Or is this just a panic attack?* He tried to stay as calm and still as possible, consciously focusing on slowing his breathing and heart rate. It didn't matter. His breathing was starting to come in gulps and he felt himself begin to swoon as he gasped for air.

There were noises somewhere outside the box he was in, but they sounded distant, almost as if he was hearing them through a long tunnel. He wasn't sure if he heard voices. *Was that a gunshot?* He felt either a drop of condensation or a tear run down his face. *I'm running out of time...I need to get out.* Panic attack or not, Gooby felt like his time was running out and one way or another, he couldn't stand to be in this box a second longer. Within the smooth, steel box Gooby began to thrash as violently as he could. Kicking, screaming, and pounding his fists feebly against the unforgiving, cold steel. His breathing was coming in fits and starts. He began to feel as if he was choking on his own tongue. He wanted to find his cell phone one more time, to call the guys for help. His fingers fumbled in the dark. They felt fat and numb. He wasn't sure he was feeling anything with them. *Damn it*, he thought. *Where is that phone?* His brain seemed foggy. *Is it in my pocket, or did I leave it next to me?*

Although it was black as ink inside the box, he began to see a gold-flecked haze closing in around the edges of his vision. He could no longer move his limbs. Exhausted, barely able to suck in a breath, he felt himself begin to drift and then the tears did stream down his temples in salty lines. He relaxed and felt himself floating, spinning, almost like the bed spins he remembered having after a drunken night in college, but this was gentler and not at all nauseating. It was as if he was being gently rocked to sleep on slowly rolling waves.

34
Cooper

Chuck and I looked at each other and moved in the same direction, almost in unison. Forward, away from the light and the hallway. We passed patient rooms with names still outside the doors—boxes of papers and charts lined the hallway. An empty gurney stood outside room B231 waiting for Stanwick, Agnes B., who had long since departed this ward and possibly this world. Thank God no one names their kids Agnes anymore. If my wife had been named Agnes, I don't think I would have ever considered marrying her. The sounds of small, scurrying rodents arose in our wake. I'm sure that the empty parts of the hospital had given shelter to a myriad of urban wildlife in the five years since it closed.

As we walked quickly through the empty ward, my imagination created ghosts of what this unit must have been like when it was full of life, and death, the incessant beeping of monitors filling the air. The scurrying mice replaced by scurrying orderlies and nurses. The smells of bland food and bodily fluids mixed together filled my memory. They say that smells trigger your memory more strongly than anything else. In this case, just thinking about the smells of a hospital had triggered memories of visiting my grandparents here years ago. Hospitals were supposed to be antiseptic and clean, but rarely do they ever smell that way.

Instead of the boxes in the hall, I imagined patient's families conferring in whispers with the wizened, kindly old doctors who had come to break the news of their loved one's diagnosis. Nervous young residents trying to appear confident as they discussed their oh-so-clinical impressions with their mentors, listing symptoms, vital signs, and lab results, not in the hope that their numbers or assessments would save a life, but that they would impress enough to get them a shot at assisting on a really good surgery.

The gurney in my imagination was no longer empty and moved slowly down the hall past me, carrying a fifty-something woman on her way to some unknown procedure. Although it was only my imagination coloring in the empty ward, I still looked away uncomfortably. My fear of death was never far from the surface. For as long as I could remember, I had avoided eye contact with patients in wheel chairs and hospital beds, even my own family members.

Even their illnesses seized me with a terror that I was surely very poor at hiding. I was fearful of touching them. When my grandparents had passed away in this very hospital, I had stood uncomfortably at their bedside, wanting to say goodbye with a kiss and a hug to match the thousands they had conferred upon me over my lifetime, but I was unable to. Somehow I believed that if I made eye contact or touched someone in the hospital I might be contaminated, infected by whatever horrible affliction had beset them. I know that my fear is completely unfounded, but as a therapist, I also know that the logical part of our brain rarely wins the arguments with the emotional part of our brain.

As we rounded the corner in the hallway, we were both relieved to be at least out of a direct line of sight from our pursuers, but that sense of relief passed quickly as, in the distance, we could hear the double doors slam shut. Someone else had entered the ward. Around the corner we had turned, the hallway ended just ahead with the entrance to a stairwell. I was just about to break into a full, terror-induced sprint towards the door when Chuck firmly took my shoulder and guided me towards the door of a patient's room. After I stepped out of the hallway and into the empty, musty, dark room, Chuck motioned for me to stay as if I was the family dog. I may have mentioned this before, but it bears repeating, *he is so going to get his ass kicked when all this is over*. Right now I'm thinking that Gooby may be the lucky one because he doesn't have to deal with this shit.

Chuck stepped out into the hallway and towards the stairwell door. No hail of gunfire broke out, so that was at least one step in the right direction. As Chuck stepped out of my sight I was seized with panic, thinking that he was leaving me behind. A few seconds later when I heard the large, metal door to the stairs slam shut, I was certain he had left me to be discovered. As I moved toward the door, gun raised, Chuck rushed back into the room and pushed me backward, away from the door with his finger held to his lips in the international sign for "Shush!" I obeyed and as we both stood in the darkened room, we heard the sound of footsteps begin to build to a crescendo, peaking in speed and volume as they reached our end of the hallway and sped past our hiding place.

It sounded like at least two of them. As we waited, my heart pounded in my chest so fast and hard I was fearful it could be heard outside the room. To me, my tension was palpable and I was afraid that, even in the dim light, Chuck could see how completely out of my element I was. I tried imagining how to look calm and confident, but I was sure I was failing miserably. Even my trademark wit had left me for the moment. I'm not sure if I was, but it sure as hell felt like I was holding my breath. This situation reminded me of all those nights as a young child that I would wake up seized with fear from a nightmare and certain that Freddie Krueger or Jason was in my room ready to pounce if I moved or breathed. Remember that belief we all had? The one that said that if we were under the covers and didn't move the monsters couldn't see us? Unfortunately, right now, I had no covers to hide under and we weren't about to wake up from this nightmare.

The footsteps definitely passed the room we were in, the darkness apparently concealing any evidence that we had taken a detour. A voice shouted in a whisper, "C'mon, this way!" I knew that voice. It was our friend Jimmy's dad, from down the street. He may have been older, but he didn't sound any different than he did when I was a kid and he yelled at us for stealing a few Playboy magazines from his stash in the basement. I still remember how we tried to suppress our smirks at his attempt to chastise us for this.

A few seconds later, the door to the stairwell slammed shut once again and the footsteps receded—up or down we couldn't tell. My shoulders relaxed and I began to breathe again. To my relief I could see Chuck relax a little too. We began to slowly edge our way towards the hall, ears alert for the sound of anyone else. Chuck was taking the lead of course, and that was fine with me. Chuck moved forward, gun slowly sweeping back and forth in front of him. I had my gun up; pointed toward the ceiling, afraid of shooting Chuck in the back if I sneezed or panicked in some way. As Chuck reached the door of the room and slowly peered into the hallway, I passed the room's bathroom on my right. Paranoid, my nerves on edge, I saw something in my peripheral vision. As I turned to the bathroom it felt as if a thousand volts of electricity shot through every inch of my body at once. There, in the darkness of the bathroom, was the shadowy figure of a man. Without a thought I turned and fired three shots into his chest. With the silencer on it sounded like a hard expulsion of air, like something had been punctured, followed by three small thuds as the bullets hit their mark. The body fell over and Chuck was immediately behind my left shoulder, gun drawn and ready.

I had never shot at anyone before, but I was relieved to know that even though I was nervous, I had done what needed to be done and did so accurately and as sharp as anyone I had seen on C.S.I. As I mentally patted myself on the back, Chuck moved past me and into the bathroom. He withdrew a small, pen-sized flashlight from his pocket and a bright, thin line of light illuminated the scene before him. In the tight confines of the small bathroom the tiny light was more than enough illumination to reveal a scene I hadn't expected.

Chuck crouched down to examine the body and as he did so, he turned to look over his shoulder at me and whispered, "Nice shooting, MacGyver. That's one CPR mannequin that won't be bothering anyone else for a long time."

Asshole. I don't think MacGyver even carried a gun. But he was right—I had shot a CPR mannequin that had perhaps been left sitting on the toilet as a joke by some hospital employee as they left the building for the last time. For five years that mannequin had sat there, taking an imaginary crap, until I had shown up tonight and blasted it into oblivion.

34

Chuck called his buddies back at the office. *It must be nice to have spies at your beck and call 24/7, I thought, especially ones with the technology these guys seemed to have at their fingertips.* Using the signal from Gooby's cell phone, they had pinpointed his location for us. He was thirty feet down from where we were, making it the first floor, and about two hundred feet due west of us. Unfortunately, in the maze that passed for hospital hallways, there was no path that would take us in a straight line for two hundred feet.

Getting to the first floor would be easy enough if our pursuers weren't waiting at the bottom of the stairs for us. Chuck and I were all too aware of the time that had passed since we last spoke to Goob. Hopefully it wasn't too late. We crept out into the hallway. Our pursuers had left the eerie stillness of the abandoned ward in their wake. We seemed to be alone again, and as far as we knew, no one knew where we were. We eased open the door at the top of the stairs and carefully returned it to rest, cringing at even the smallest sound. Cat-like, or so I imagined, we crept down the stairs, pointing our guns ahead of us and around each corner as we descended.

Chuck pushed the door open just an inch, listening intently for at least half a minute before pushing it open far enough for us to step through. I trusted Chuck to lead us in the right direction, because frankly, once we got indoors, I had no freaking idea what direction west was. There were no lights on in this part of the hospital and it looked as abandoned as the ward we had just left. By the signs that were still posted we appeared to be heading in the direction of the cafeteria, the oncology department, and the palliative care unit, otherwise known as death's waiting room. It hardly seemed fair that people who were dying had to put up with the smell of hospital food all day.

As we passed the hallway to the palliative care unit, I could see that it was a very nicely decorated, almost a cozy ward, that had been designed with the comfort of the dying and their families in mind. Lush, green carpet covered the floor and dark paneling lined the hallway. I shuddered a little as we passed the entrance to the unit. If any place in the hospital held the ghosts that I had imagined earlier, this was it. As nice as it seemed for a hospital ward, I hope I don't finish out my final days in a place like this, acutely aware that with each passing day my life is slowly expiring. If I ever die, I want it to be quick and such a surprise that I don't even know it happens. Well, that, or just drifting away while in a dream, sleeping in the comfort of my own bed. Most of all, I knew that I didn't want to be dead tonight, but I was all too aware that was entirely a possibility.

I looked into rooms as we crept along carefully. Unlike the rest of the hospital, the rooms in this ward looked as if they had very recently held patients. As I glanced into a room, I saw a fully made-up bed, and slightly more disturbing, four-point restraints attached to each bed. From my days of evaluating psychiatric patients in the E.R., I recognized the four leather loops attached to each corner of the bed that in days gone by were intended to secure patients that were likely to be a danger to themselves or others. In a palliative care unit they seemed highly out of place. Why would there be freshly made beds here? And why would patients on this unit, patients who were usually weak with a terminal illness, need to be tied down? Something wasn't right here.

We continued following the blue line on the floor until it ended at a "T" with a yellow line going to the right and a red line going to the left. The oncology unit was to the right and the sign indicated that the cafeteria was down the hallway to the left. Not knowing why, I gestured to the left. It was just a feeling, or maybe I was just hungry. Following the red line somehow seemed appropriate tonight. Red was the universal color for danger, and we had seemingly gone looking for danger tonight. Thus far we had been stupendously successful in our quest, so why stop now? Besides, if we were going to rescue Gooby, we were going to have to walk further into the lion's den. Chuck shrugged his shoulders and we headed in that direction. Other than our own movements, the silence was again almost smothering, heavy. According to Chuck we were now headed south, so we needed to find a turn that would again take us west.

After about thirty feet there was indeed a hallway that went off to our right, west. There was no colored line on the floor; no signs telling us what might be at the end of the hallway. The doors of the cafeteria were clearly ahead of us in the direction we had been going along the red line.

The hallway heading west was filled with an inky darkness so thick it appeared that it would feel heavy if you were to touch it—as if it might swallow you whole and suffocate you if you stepped into it. The gloomy light from the hallway we were in didn't seem to extend very far down this hallway, as if even the light was afraid to go any further. I knew that all of these thoughts were my fevered imagination working overtime, but I also knew in my gut that this hallway was without a doubt where we needed to go. Then, echoing through the hallways we heard, "Warriors, come out and pla-ay!" Shit. We had no choice—we had to go forward now. This hallway was our best bet to stay out of sight.

With little hesitation, Chuck stepped past me and once again swept his penlight in front of us, the beam penetrating the darkness for a short distance before it too was engulfed. We advanced slowly, step by step, with the tiny electric torch revealing bare, ordinary walls. I relaxed a little as I realized that there was nothing any more sinister here than a really dark hallway in an old building. We had gone perhaps twenty feet, maybe a little more, when, in the dim light of Chuck's tiny flashlight, I saw it.

Tucked away in a small recess, around a corner and behind a vending machine, is a door. By today's standards it appears unusual. It is not exceptional in its shape or other dimensions, but it is distinctly different in a way that is difficult to define. The door is made of wood, as are many doors. The grain of the wood creates an intricate spiral pattern visible through the amber finish. In the nearly abandoned institutional setting, however, the wooden door seems out of place when compared with the more modern steel and glass sections of the edifice that contains it. The brass, bulb-style handle appears to be far out of place, an ornament from another time.

The broad, windowless door serves as the dead end of a short, dark alcove. There is no light to brighten this exaggerated cubby—no windows nearby and no glowing globe hanging from the ceiling. It is as if the architects intended it to be ignored. The door is almost hidden in plain sight. Although the nearby vending machine must certainly attract regular traffic, the floor in front of the door appears to be thick with the gray dust that always seems to coat the hallways of buildings usually referred to as institutions. It has the smell you recognize from the time you secretly found your way into the boiler room of your elementary school all those years ago. It is a smell that tells you that you are alone in a place entered rarely and only by necessity.

Centered directly above the door, mounted so that it points straight out from the wall, is a basic light fixture containing a single, bare, red bulb. The red light is not illuminated, nor does it appear to have been in quite some time. What could the red light be intended as a warning for? A swath of dim light from the nearby hallway reluctantly edges its way into the entryway. It is by this dim light that I am able to make out two details that had escaped my notice at first glance. On the wall to the left of the oddly imposing door is a switch in the down position. In the gloomy light I am also able to see that there is a single word stenciled on the door at about eye level. The letters are gold and of a font that appears to be quite old.

"Necropsy" it simply says. Behind the door is death, or at least this is where death used to be when this was a functioning hospital. Death may yet be awaiting me on the other side of this door.

The room behind the mysterious door is the old morgue. I tentatively reach out to try the knob, not sure if I really want it to turn. The brass handle refuses to budge and in my mind I feel a relief that I hope isn't apparent on my face. On a whim, I flip the switch to my left. Nothing happens. No sound from within the room. No red light suddenly ablaze above me. No blaring alarms to warn anyone of an intruder. What could the switch be for? As I look to the space at the bottom of the door expecting to see a sliver of light from within, I instead see something that seems to make my blood freeze in my veins. At first I am unsure if it is just a shadow, but as I bend down to look more closely, I see that it is indeed what I feared it might be.

A footprint, or rather, half of a footprint. The other half I assume is on the other side of the door. All that is visible is the imprint of a heel in the dust. It is barely visible, but a distinct impression is definitely there. Someone had entered this locked door in the very recent past.

The hospital hadn't been open, save for a few isolated outpatient offices in another wing, in five years. The one-hundred-year-old institution had been a victim of poor financial planning and, at the end, a scandal resulting from a contamination of the hospital's water system with the bacteria that causes Legionnaire's Disease. Some of the victims of that outbreak had no doubt had their autopsies performed in the room I now desperately knew I must find a way into. A week ago I could not have conceived of the series of events that caused me to question virtually everything I thought I knew about my life and brought me to this door.

35

"Coop, here, try this. I've got your back." Chuck handed me a small, elongated, thin, metal casing and his penlight. The small metal case opened flat to reveal several, approximately three-inch-long, jagged-shaped pieces of some kind of sturdy metal inside. Lock picks. Chuck wanted me to try to break into the old morgue while he stood guard a few feet away. I suppose that's better than leaving me to protect his back. Unless we were attacked by a pack of crazed mannequins, I was probably more dangerous to him than anything else. I tucked my gun into the front of my pants, hoping that I wouldn't accidently blow my dick clean off if I tripped or something.

Holding the flashlight in my mouth, I aimed it at the ancient doorknob and began to fumble with the variety of lock picks. "Shit!" I said as I dropped the whole set and they clattered noisily to the ground. If there were anyone inside this room, our chances of surprising them had just vanished. I froze for a moment, listening. There was no sound. We appeared to be as alone in this hallway as it first seemed. I tried one pick and then another with no success. I didn't know if I was even using them right. I was about to turn to Chuck to suggest that he take over when a familiar smell hit my nostrils. It was a sweet, sticky smell that seemed so out of context that I couldn't quite place it at first. Then, as realization dawned on me, I felt my heart stop. Halls Cherry Cough Drops.

I slowly turned around, penlight still in my mouth. The little circle of light revealed Chuck, but behind him was Cliff, with a gun pointed at his head. It may have been a trick of the light, or my imagination, but I thought I could see him smiling, almost like a predator baring his sharp teeth before pouncing on his prey. Chuck was wisely not moving, but I could see the look of panic in his eyes as Cliff carefully, gun still pointing at his temple, took the gun from Chuck's hand and tucked it into the back of his pants. My gun was still tucked into the front of my pants—I didn't think that Cliff could see it as long as I was still facing the door and kept the penlight focused away from my body. I was in stunned disbelief. My head felt numb.

Cliff whispered in a hiss, "Get that the fuck open and get inside, and Chuck, don't even think about moving." My mouth felt dry as the penlight hung there. Cliff couldn't be serious. He couldn't kill us. Wouldn't kill us. I had to believe that was true. Even if he was one of them and had been his whole life, he had also been one of us his whole life. That had to mean something. "Cooper! Stop standing there and unlock the door," he growled at me.

I turned towards the door again, moving carefully, not knowing if a single move might get me or Chuck a bullet in our heads. I tried another pick in the door and this one slid in cleanly. As I jiggled it around, I heard the cylinders quietly click into place and I tried the knob. This time it turned in my hand and I looked back over my shoulder. The gun was still trained on Chuck's head. Cliff nodded at me and I pushed the door slowly open in front of me. As I pushed it and began to move forward, it occurred to me that I had never seen the inside of a morgue before. Then again, how many do see the inside of a morgue when they've still got a heartbeat? I had seen them on television and in movies of course, but this large, open room was nothing like the modern, antiseptic, gleaming, stainless-steel rooms I had seen on the big screen. It also immediately occurred to me that I had never smelled a morgue before and no one on television seemed to be plugging their noses as they worked in their morgues. The smell that hit me as the door quietly swung slowly open wasn't good, but it also wasn't what I feared it might be. There was no smell of death or bodily fluids. No rancid, reeking odor of decay, just the smell of a room that had gotten far too little fresh air over the past several years. Maybe it was my imagination, but the room had a slight chill to it, just a few degrees cooler than the rest of the hospital, but noticeable.

"Keep facing forward until I tell you differently," Cliff growled at us, "and keep your hands in front of you." His voice sounded casual, almost conversational, as it echoed in the nearly empty room. It was weird. My thoughts still raced, with Chuck disarmed I knew I was going to have to be the one to take the shot, to kill one of my best friends. And I knew it had to be soon. Gooby was in one of these drawers, possibly suffocating. Something had to give, and soon. I glanced around without moving my head. My eyes strained in the darkness to get the layout of the room, looking for possible weapons, escape routes, or anything I could use to my advantage. I heard the shuffling of feet behind me. Not sure if it was Cliff or Chuck, I stayed still as my eyes adjusted to the dim light. I could see a wall of metal drawers that, with exception of a little dust and tarnish, looked as if they could still be used. I wondered which one Gooby was in and I also wondered if I was about to end up in one as well.

A click was immediately followed by the flicker of aged fluorescent lights overhead. Only a few still worked and their light was enough for me to get a better look at the room. It was square with no other entrances or exits other than the one we had come in. A tall metal cabinet stood open and empty to the left. There was a desk against the right wall, and a long rectangular examination table in the center of the room. The floor was basic institutional tiles, slippery with dust. And then I saw what I was looking for. On the floor in front of one of the drawers were footprints. The handle of this drawer gleamed ever so slightly in the dimly flickering white light. It had been used recently. That had to be where Gooby was.

Cliff still hadn't done anything other than point the gun, and hadn't said anything else since we entered the morgue. What was he waiting for? Could this pause possibly be him hesitating because he was nervous or ambivalent about the position he had his former friends in? If so, I have to use that to my advantage. It might be the only advantage I have right now. "Cliff, c'mon, let us turn around and talk to you. You know this isn't right. Put the gun down," I said, trying to sound as if I was scared and pleading with him. I heard a sigh, barely perceptible, but it was there. He sounded as if he might be letting his guard down. I wasn't touching Chuck, but I could sense him tensing as he stood next to me. He sensed the same thing I did.

"No, I can't do that," Cliff finally answered. "You guys should have never come here. You should have stayed out of it." Then I startled as I heard the door open behind us.

"He's right you know," the new voice said. "You're fools just like your fathers. You can turn around. There are no secrets here any longer." Cliff's father sounded smug, sarcastic, almost like he was mocking us. *What I wouldn't give to knock that look off his face*, I thought.

As Chuck and I turned around slowly and carefully I said, "Jeffrey Warren, I presume?" And just like that, for a fleeting moment, the smug look was replaced by doubt in his eyes as if I had just slapped him.

He quickly regained a placid look as he walked towards me and said, "Cooper, I'm surprised a smart guy like you didn't figure out who I was years ago. And it's too bad too because if I'd had the chance to educate you like I have Cliff and all my other followers you could have been a tremendous asset to *The Tribe*." His face was only inches from mine as he sneered. His eyes met mine and he reached into the waist of my jeans and pulled out my gun. "It's also too bad your father wasn't as smart as you, or we could have remained friends." He tucked the gun into the back of his pants and turned to Cliff, "Kill them."

There were at least three people in that room whose faces immediately registered a look of panic. My eyes darted from Chuck to Cliff and back. Chucks eyes ran the same gauntlet while Cliff's eyes made the rounds as well before he regained his steely composure. For just a moment I had seen a look of doubt in Cliff's eyes. He was scared. I knew it. He couldn't do this. "Well, Cliff," his father said, "you heard me. Kill them. Now. You had your chances before, and if you screw this one up, I'll do it myself and you'll go with them."

Cliff raised his gun and again pointed it at us. Back and forth it swayed, first trained on Chuck briefly and then over to me. My mind raced trying to think of some way to make a move without getting one of us shot. Who was I kidding? My moves here were likely to be about as smooth as my moves on the dance floor at a wedding reception. Embarrassingly bad. Of course when I was dancing my wife only wished I was dead. But what the hell was Chuck doing?

He's the Spy Guy, I thought. *Why can't he do some James Bond or Jackie Chan shit and get us out of this?* Unfortunately, this was real life and movie stunts don't work here.

That's when Cliff finally spoke, and as he did so he lowered his gun. "No Dad. I can't do it. These guys are my friends."

Jeffrey Warren looked down at the floor and shook his head, letting out a sigh. "Well Clifford, I'm sorry it had to come to this," he said as he pulled the gun out of the waist of his jeans and pointed it at me.

In the blink of an eye, Cliff raised his gun again, but this time he pointed it at his father. "No Dad, this is where it ends. Put your gun down." My heart leapt. I was going to get out of this alive—or was I? Jeffrey Warren did not put his gun down. It remained aimed at my head.

He chuckled, "Clifford, after all this time you're finally going to stand up to me? Over these two? You don't have the balls. You know what *The Tribe* will do to you."

Cliff appeared to be gritting his teeth as he spoke, the gun pointed at his father, shaking in his tense, white-knuckled hand. I could see his fingers squeezing the trigger ever so slightly. "No Dad, it's over." As the two shots rang out, I threw myself to the floor. Or was I hit? Droplets of blood sprayed everywhere as Jeffrey Warren's hand exploded. The gun clattered heavily to the floor.

As I fell to the floor, I could feel a line of searing heat across my temple. I landed heavily on my side, badly cracking my elbow on the cold, tiled floor. On the floor in front of me was the gun. I quickly scooped it up and immediately trained it on Jeffrey Warren, who was helplessly clutching his newly ventilated right hand. "Don't fucking move," I growled. The gun was slippery with his blood, but suddenly it didn't feel as heavy in my hand as it had before. "Chuck, get Goob," I shouted, without taking my eyes off my wounded prey.

36

Quicker than Chuck could react, Cliff ran over to the drawer, released the latch, and pulled it open. He slid one arm under Gooby's neck, one under his legs, lifted him out, and lowered him to the floor. I spared a glance. It didn't look good. Gooby's face appeared to be a pale, whitish-blue, and in the dim light I couldn't tell if his chest was rising and falling.

Cliff began mouth to mouth immediately, hand behind the neck, head tilted back, and nose pinched, just like we had all learned in Boy Scouts, health class, or somewhere else. "C'mon Goob! What the hell are you doing?" he shouted in between breaths. Goob's chest rose and fell as Cliff filled his lungs. I began to feel the warmth of my own blood running down the side of my face from where the bullet had grazed me. I kept the gun trained on Jeffrey Warren although at this point, one handed and losing blood, he probably wasn't much of a threat.

"C'mon Goob. You are not going to die. This is not going to be my fault!" He was almost shouting and sobbing between breaths into Gooby's lungs. I began to wonder how long before we should give up. How much mouth to mouth was enough before we realized he was gone? In the meantime, Chuck had called for an ambulance and backup from his department.

SLAM! The door flew open, hitting the wall and echoing around the room. We all turned. Cliff paused to lift his eyes, but stayed intent on trying to breathe life back into Gooby if he could. Amidst some struggling and scuffling we saw one of Jeffrey Warren's henchmen, our old friend Jimmy's dad, drag Maria into the room, his arm around her neck and shoulders and a gun trained at her head. "You, put the gun down on the floor and step away from it."

Just then, something snapped inside my brain. This was the point where the day's overload of stress took away all rational thought. I did not put the gun down on the floor. "Oh for fuck's sake!" I shouted as I threw my hands in the air. 'This is abso-fucking-lutely ridiculous! Are you freaking kidding me? I can't take any more! A week ago I was just living a normal life, minding my own fucking business, when my friend's dad passed away, normally I thought. Since then I've barely had time to grab a fucking snack in between you assholes trying to kill me and just about anyone else who crosses your path. What the *hell* is wrong with you people?" I continued to stomp about the room, my voice at the top of my lungs and showing no signs of letting up. Everyone in the room, mouths agape, just stared at me. The guy with the gun appeared a little nervous and hadn't let down his guard yet.

"This is bullshit. This is absolute bullshit!" At that moment Jeffrey Warren, I couldn't think of him as Cliff's dad anymore, started to struggle to his feet. I flew around and pointed the gun at him again. "Sit down, asshole. You are *not* going anywhere. And Mr. Schwarz, what the hell is your problem?" I shouted as I turned in his direction and began to walk towards him. He and everyone else appeared mesmerized by my tirade, almost forgetting the reality of the situation. They were watching me as if I were a crazy person on the street walking around shouting at demons only I could see.

"You have a son. He was our friend. You helped me when I wiped out on my bike and got my hand all cut up in front of your house that time. What the *fuck* is wrong with all of you? This is the fucking 21st century! Nobody lives like this. Nobody acts like you people do!" I was really ranting now, waving my arms and stomping around as if I was in my own world.

"Oh my god! I can't tell you how much this pisses me off! Why can't you just leave people *alone*? You cannot even believe the fucking week I've had. Oh, that's right—you can—because you caused all of it. I still have to bury my father in a couple days too. Thanks for that, you *assholes*! I just want to go the *fuck* home, take a nap, and have coffee while I read the morning paper! Is that too much to ask? Is that too *fucking* much to ask?" I was close enough now. I wheeled around sharply, swung the gun up, and fired a shot into the shoulder of Mr. Schwarz. *Checkmate,* I thought to myself.

He fell away from Maria and she quickly ran behind me. Chuck ran over and grabbed the gun from his hand before he realized what had happened. With the exception of Mr. Schwarz panting as he clutched his shoulder, there was silence in the room. We all just looked around, no one quite sure what to do or what was supposed to happen next.

"Nice speech, Coop," a voice said weakly, and at that point we all turned around. "And Cliff, are you still sucking on those stupid cough drops? I'm nearly dead and I have to wake up to the smell of those cough drops and your tongue in my mouth? That ain't right." I imagine that at that moment, my grin was as wide as Cliff and Chuck's were.

37

Moments after Gooby had been revived; the reinforcements Chuck had called for burst into the room and took care of the rest. Their sweep of the building had netted two more members of *The Apocalypse Tribe* and enough evidence to put Cliff's dad away for a long time. Maria as it turned out, was innocent of any involvement with *The Apocalypse Tribe.* Her son Joshua had just been a curious kid who palmed the memory stick at Gooby's house because he thought it was interesting. And of course, we held no ill will towards our friend Cliff. We've known him since we were in diapers and would still know him when we we're all in diapers again. In the end he had made the right choice, and that was all that mattered to us.

A week later as we sat on Gooby's deck, feet up on the railing, enjoying a beer and a couple cigars, watching the sun set over our neighborhood, we weren't thinking of the funerals or the events of the week before. We were just four guys who still felt like we had never grown up.

"Guys, I don't know how you can forgive me for everything," Cliff said.

"Don't worry about it, Cliff," Gooby replied casually, just before throwing down another swig of his ice-cold beer. "That wasn't any worse than when Chuck was totally hitting on your wife when you two were engaged and you forgave him for that, right?"

Cliff literally did a spit take, spewing beer all over the deck railing in front of us. "*What*?" he sputtered.

Chuck just laughed. "Don't worry about it. I was drunk and that was a long time ago. Nothing happened. After this past week, how about we just call it even?" Cliff just shook his head.

"So Goob," Chuck began, almost cackling. "How are you and Maria doing?"

Goob just threw his head back and laughed before firing back, "Chuck, don't even start with me. You've got to be the only spy in the world who can't score chicks, so don't start busting on me."

It looked like Chuck blushed, but we can never tell with his perpetually red cheeks.

Cliff chipped in, "Hey Chuck, maybe if you keep looking you'll find another evil cult full of women who seduce men before killing them. That might be the only way you're ever going to get laid."

Chuck took it all in good-naturedly. "Well, it would be one hell of a great way to go, wouldn't it?"

Just then, from Gooby's hip we heard *The Thong Song* emanating from his cell phone.

"Oh no, Chuck," I laughed. "You didn't do that again, did you?"

Chuck shook his head and replied, "No, I swear it wasn't me this time."

Gooby just chuckled. "No, it wasn't Chuck. That's my ringtone for Maria. I'll call her later. She knows I'm with you guys."

I knew it didn't need to be said, but I said it anyway. "Well, it's about that time, isn't it?" Once again *The Walk* took us on the familiar loop of our neighborhood, bringing us right back home every time.

About the Author

Phil Taylor is a father of three, husband to one, and life-long smart ass to many. He has been well trained by his two dogs and a cat and is a loyal servant to them all. Phil plays a mean game of Ping-Pong and claims to make the best grilled cheese sandwiches in the world, bar none. He has a Master's degree in Psychology and spent many years working in the field of mental health before realizing that stringing words together might be a little bit more fun. His first fiction novel, White Picket Prisons, is an ode to the life-long friends that shaped his life.

You can follow more of Phil's work by looking him up on the interwebs at:

www.facebook.com/AuthorPhilTaylor
&

www.thephilfactor.com